DATE DUE

DEC 28 199			
JUL 0 6 199			
SEP 0 9 1994			
SEP 3 0 1998			
JUL 2 4 2003			

BONNIE PRYOR

Horses
in the
Garage

MORROW JUNIOR BOOKS

New York

Printed in the United States of America.
1 2 3 4 5 6 7 8 9 10

Library of Congress Cataloging-in-Publication Data
Pryor, Bonnie. Horses in the garage / Bonnie Pryor.   p. cm.
Summary: Sixth grader Samantha finds a way to cope with her
difficulties in adjusting to a new stepfather, a new home, and a new
school when she makes friends with the unconventional Jasmine and
learns to ride a horse. Sequel to "Rats, Spiders & Love."
ISBN 0-688-10567-X
[1. Moving, Household—Fiction. 2. Stepfathers—Fiction. 3. Family
life—Fiction. 4. Schools—Fiction. 5. Horses—Fiction.] I. Title
PZ7.P94965Hn 1992 [Fic]—dc20   92-7287   CIP AC

To Meredith Charpentier,
and to Muffin and Velvet, and
to C. J. the surprise!

CHAPTER ONE

"**S**TOP HOGGING the whole seat," Julie said, pushing Sam's legs away.

"I can't get comfortable," Sam complained, twisting to sit sideways. "My rear end is numb."

"Your rear end is going to be worse than numb if you don't get over on your side of the seat. I'm trying to read."

"Samantha, sit on your half of the seat, please." Mrs. Weirton interrupted the war between her daughters before it came to blows.

"Can't we stop soon? I'm thirsty, and I have to go to the bathroom." Samantha knew she sounded whiny, but she couldn't help it. After three days of driving across the country, she was bored and cranky.

Jim Weirton, her new stepfather, sounded grim. "That's all I've heard all day long. If we keep stopping every five minutes, we'll never get there. I made my travel plan with enough stops for anyone."

The girls looked at each other, reunited by their common plight. Their stepfather was a man who believed in organization and lists. All the way across the country they had adhered to his travel plan: drive for three hours, then take a fifteen-minute break.

"Sam, get a can of pop from the cooler," said her mother. "And why don't you read your book for a while?"

"Reading makes me carsick," Samantha said. She stared out the window at the flat, monotonous scenery. It was one thing to look at a map of the United States in social studies class and say that it was a big country. But driving from her old home in Oregon to her new home in Ohio made her understand just how vast the country really was.

Julie closed her book and brushed the hair out of her eyes. Even after three days locked in the car, she looked fresh and pretty. But her lips turned down in a pouty frown every time she looked at her stepfather. Samantha patted her own hair. She didn't need a mirror to know it was limp and lifeless.

"I don't know why we couldn't have flown," Julie grumbled. "It would only have taken a few hours."

"Because," her mother answered, "we had to bring the car. And I thought it would be nice to have this time together as a family."

"That might have been all right if *she* wasn't in the car," Julie said. Left unspoken, but obvious from her looks, was a similar wish for Jim to disappear.

Julie pushed Samantha's leg off the middle of the seat, where she had stretched it. "Why couldn't you have made me an only child?" she snarled.

Samantha glared at her sister. "If there was an only child, it wouldn't have been you. I was born first."

"You two sound like a couple of three-year-olds back there," their mother said. "And neither one of you would be here if I had only had one child. Kevin's the oldest, you know."

The girls' older brother, Kevin, had remained behind to attend college. Even though Samantha thought she would never miss him, she found that she already did. It seemed strange to think that Kevin wouldn't be part of the new household. He would join them for a few weeks at Christmas, but Samantha knew it would never be quite the same.

"We'll stop soon," Jim said, flashing them a smile in the rearview mirror. "And later tonight you'll see your new house."

"Tell me about it," Samantha said, even though she had heard it all before. Jim and her mother had gone to Ohio on their honeymoon and purchased the house so the family could be settled before the school year started. That was when Julie's antagonism had begun. Previously she had been thrilled with the idea of a new stepfather.

"I don't know why we couldn't go," Julie had complained every day while her mother and Jim were gone.

"They're on their honeymoon, dummy," Sam had answered once. "Kids don't go on honeymoons."

"I thought Jim would pay attention to us. Instead, now we don't even have a mother."

"Of course we have a mother. She'll be back in two weeks."

"And then you will all live happily ever after." Kevin had tried to tease Julie out of her miserable mood.

But Julie refused to be kidded out of her mood. "Humph," she had snorted. "Next he'll probably send us away to boarding school."

Although Sam had been irritated by her sister's surliness, she had secretly harbored the same thoughts. "I know he would never send us away like Julie says," she had told her best friend, Sara. "But it does seem like he's all Mom thinks about anymore. If they are not kissing and hugging, they're looking at each other with goo-goo eyes."

"I think it's terribly romantic," Sara had said.

"At their age it's terribly disgusting. They should have more dignity," Sam had retorted.

"Bakerstown is a nice little town," Jim said, breaking into her thoughts. He flashed her a sympathetic smile. "Of course, you'll be trading an ocean view for rolling hills and green fields, but I think when you get used to that, you'll like it. Our house is a couple of miles from town, but the bus will pick you up right in front for school."

At the mention of school, Samantha's stomach did a queer little flip. Moving was hard enough. Starting the first year of middle school in a new place would be a nightmare. "What if no one likes me?" she asked.

"What's not to like?" Jim said. "A girl who raises rats and discovers a new kind of spider ought to be very popular."

He was teasing, but Samantha blushed, remembering how hard she had tried to keep Jim from marrying her mother. She had chosen the rats as a science project, knowing that Jim was allergic to animals. But later, after switching her project to spiders, she had discovered a green one that no one had ever named before. She had even had a brief moment of fame on the local news.

"You'd better not talk about spiders in middle school," Julie said. "You don't want to start off with people thinking you're weird."

Their mother twisted around in her seat. "There's nothing wrong with being interested in nature."

"Middle school is different. It's not like the old days when you went to school. You can talk about stuff like that at home. But if you want to be popular, you can't go around talking about bugs."

Jim winked at Mom. "You remember the old days, don't you? We rode to school in covered wagons."

"How do you know so much about middle school?" Sam asked her sister. "You are only going to be a fifth-grade baby."

"I used to talk with my friend Tessa's big sister. She told me all about it," Julie said smugly. "I plan on being prepared when I go."

In spite of herself, Sam had to ask. "So what do they talk about?"

Julie shrugged. "Boys. Clothes. Stuff like that."

Sam scrunched miserably in the corner. Boys.

Last year in school she had been friends with a boy named Harold. But she knew that wasn't what Julie meant. There was a difference between being friends with a boy and having a boyfriend. The subject of clothes was even worse. She was much more comfortable in a pair of jeans and a T-shirt than anything else. Sitting around talking about the latest fashions sounded pretty boring.

"Just be yourself," Jim offered. "You'll do all right." He twisted around and smiled. "*I* like you."

"Wait until you see our new house," Mom said, trying to cheer her up. "You'll love it. There are ten acres with it, and part of that is a lovely woods."

Sam imagined herself walking through the woods with Buffy, the family dog. "I miss Buffy," she said. "I don't know why he couldn't have come with us."

Mrs. Weirton scolded, but her eyes were sympathetic. "Kevin will bring Buffy when he comes home for Christmas. We've been all through this. You know Jim couldn't have been locked up in a car with a dog because of his allergies."

"I just said I missed him," Sam said. "You don't have to get all mad."

Mrs. Weirton sighed and faced the front again. Jim was silent, and Sam wondered if she had hurt his feelings by complaining like that. It wasn't his fault he was allergic to dogs. But knowing that didn't make it easier to leave Buffy behind.

"With all that land, maybe we could have a horse," she said. As soon as the words were out of her mouth, she regretted them. Julie gave her a sharp poke in the ribs and a withering look. "What a worm brain," she muttered under her breath.

Sam had been trying to change the subject, and instead she had reminded Jim again about his allergies. But to her surprise, he didn't seem offended.

"We might think about it. But if we did get a horse, you girls would have to take care of it. I couldn't be around one without sneezing."

Even Mom looked surprised. "But the place doesn't have a barn or even a fence," she protested.

"We can always build a barn," Jim said. He and Mom conversed quietly, discussing the possibility. Samantha exchanged an excited look with her sister, their animosity toward Jim forgotten for the moment. Having a horse might make leaving her friends and starting a new school less difficult to bear. She closed her eyes and pictured herself astride a horse. He would be black, of course. A stallion, like the one in the Walter Farley books she had read. He would be wild with everyone else, but with her, he would be gentle. Together they would explore the woods and race across the fields. The wind would whip her hair across her face, but she would urge him on and on, feeling the muscles rippling beneath her as he put on a fresh burst of speed. Samantha settled back in her seat and sighed with pleasure. She was so busy dreaming that she hardly noticed the Welcome to Ohio sign when they passed it.

For weeks she had been trying to pretend she was happy about moving, especially for her mother's sake. Mrs. Weirton had been a widow for three years after Sam's father had been killed in an auto accident, and it was nice to see her happy and smiling again. Sam looked at Jim, who was still chatting easily with her mother. He was a nice person, and she liked him in spite of the fact that he took all her mother's attention. Her mother's newfound happiness didn't make moving any easier. But a horse! That was something she hadn't imagined possible in her wildest dreams. Maybe moving across the country wouldn't be so bad after all.

"Still have to go to the bathroom?" Jim asked.

"No. I can wait until your scheduled stop," Sam said.

Jim pulled up to a service station and stopped the car. "Really, I can wait," Sam told him.

Jim smiled a bit sheepishly. "I can't," he said.

CHAPTER TWO

SAM WANTED to be the first to catch a glimpse of the new house. Her mother had showed them a photograph of it. The builders were just putting in the final touches when her parents purchased the house. So Mom and Jim had been able to pick out wallpaper and paint. Leaving the workers to finish the interior, they went back to Oregon to sell the old house and get ready to move. They even arranged for a local furniture store to deliver some new furniture and new rugs before they arrived. It would seem strange to be surrounded by everything new, Sam thought, as she strained to see the dark countryside. In spite of her intentions, the scores of small towns blurred into a weary sameness, and she fell asleep sitting up, with her head bouncing against the window. Long after midnight she jumped at her mother's gentle shake and rubbed her neck.

"We're here," Mom said softly.

The family stumbled from the car, stretching to relieve cramped muscles. It was too dark to see more than the outline of the house and an inky black line Sam decided must be the edge of the woods Mom had mentioned. Sam inhaled the dry air of late August, missing the ocean tang she had grown to love on the West Coast. The air was warm, but it carried the sharpness of early autumn.

"I'll bring in the sleeping bags from the trunk," Jim said. "Let's worry about unpacking the rest of the car tomorrow."

He unlocked the door of the house, fumbling with the key, and flipped on the lights. "Taa-daa!" he sang.

Sam and Julie crowded in, staring at their new home. The walls still smelled of fresh paint. With only the barest essentials of furniture, the room looked cold and empty. But the solid wood beams across the ceiling added a bit of warmth.

Julie rubbed her eyes. "Where's my room?"

"Upstairs," Jim said. "I'll show you. We'll have to

11

rough it a little tonight," he explained as they walked up the stairs. "Tomorrow the movers will be here with all our personal belongings. But in the meantime you can just roll out the sleeping bags on your new beds."

Most of the old furniture hadn't been worth the expense of shipping. But their clothes and a few items of furniture they couldn't bear to lose were being shipped.

"It doesn't seem right without Kevin here," Sam said.

Mrs. Weirton gave her a squeeze. "I miss him, too. But there are four bedrooms. Kevin will always have a place with us when he gets a break from school."

"This is your bedroom," Jim told Julie, turning on the lights of the first bedroom. It was painted a pale lavender, Julie's favorite color. Except for a bed, the room was bare.

Julie took her sleeping bag from Jim and rolled it out on the bed. "I'll look at it in the morning," she mumbled, flopping down. "G'night."

"And this one is yours," Jim said, opening the door to the second room. "We can switch tomorrow if it doesn't suit you," he said when Sam didn't speak, "but your Mom and I thought you would like this one. Your window looks out over the woods. You might see a deer sometime. There are lots of them around here."

"It's great," Sam answered quickly. The walls were a pale blue, and one wall was papered with pale silver unicorns. "It's more than great. It's beautiful." She hugged her mother and gave Jim an awkward kiss on his cheek, still not used to having a new father.

When Mom and Jim closed the door to their room across the hall, Sam collapsed on the new bed. There was a hollowness inside her somewhere. The bed felt strange and uncomfortable, just like everything else. Hot tears of self-pity burned in her eyes, and she brushed them away with the back of her hand. She got up and pushed open the window to look out, trying not to think about her friends back home.

The moonlight was muffled by a thick bank of clouds, giving the trees at the edge of the yard a ghostly appearance. But that wasn't what made everything seem so foreign. It took Sam a minute to realize the difference was really the sounds. She heard crickets, millions of them, judging by the noisy din. In her old home, the pounding surf had lulled her to sleep every night.

Sam pushed the sash down and sat on her bed. She had a sudden urge to crawl in bed with her mother for comfort like she'd done when she was younger. But she couldn't do that with Jim here. He was like a wall between them. But how did you fight a kind, lovable teddy-bear sort of wall? Sam thought she'd feel awful just mentioning the fact that she wished he'd get out of the way once in a while. Especially when the person on the other side of the hall, namely her mother, acted perfectly thrilled to have him there.

Sam unzipped the sleeping bag and stretched out, not bothering to undress. She knew she could never sleep in this strange place.

But sunlight streaming through the uncurtained windows woke her a few hours later. She groaned and glanced at her watch. Only five-thirty. The house was still quiet. She squeezed her eyes shut and tried to go back to sleep. After a few minutes she gave up, rolled out of bed, and looked out the window. Jim was right. There was a lovely view of the woods. From this height she could see what looked like a trail winding back into the shadows of the trees. She slipped on her shoes and tiptoed downstairs and out the back door.

The grass was wet with dew, and there was a chilly early-morning breeze that brought goose bumps to her arms. She wished she had thought to bring her sweater, but it was still packed some-

14

where in the car. Rubbing her arms for warmth, she crossed the yard and walked into the woods, following the trail she had spotted from the window in her room.

The woods were laced with vines that twisted around the trees, making the path almost impassable in spots. Sunlight created a carpet of checkered light and dark on the forest floor. Birds chirped cheerfully overhead. The distant *rat–tat–tat* of a woodpecker drilling for insects echoed through the trees. Along the sides of the trail were ferns, and in several spots grew thickets of berry vines. A few unpicked berries still clung to the stems. They would taste wonderful next spring. Sam sat on a moss-encrusted rock and allowed her mind to wander. It would be nice to have a cabin in these woods. She could be a hermit. A hermit didn't have to worry about adjusting to a new stepfather or starting a new school without knowing anyone.

A sudden crashing noise in the brush startled her out of her thoughts. She jumped to her feet, freezing as she caught a quick glimpse of what she had heard. A few feet away was a deer. For a brief moment their eyes met. It was difficult to judge who was the most surprised. Then the doe leaped over a thicket, the white of her tail a banner of distress, and disappeared. Almost immediately another deer followed, jumping gracefully over the path behind the first.

"Now you've done it," said a cross voice above her head. Sam peered up into the shadowy green in time to see a girl about her own age swing lightly down from an overhead branch and land in front of her.

"Done wh-what?" Sam stammered.

"I've been sitting in that tree since four-thirty this morning, waiting to shoot those deer. And then you came crashing along and spoiled everything."

"You were going to shoot them?" Sam asked indignantly.

"With the camera, silly." Then Sam noticed the camera fastened to a cord around the girl's neck. "I'm a wildlife photographer."

"Are you really?" Sam asked.

"Well, not yet, I guess. But I'm going to be." The girl was tall and lanky, with deep blue eyes and even teeth. "My name is Jasmine McKenna."

"That's a neat name," Sam said.

"Doesn't really fit me. A Jasmine should be sweet and delicate, don't you think? I call myself Jazz, but my parents hate it. That's what they get for giving me such a dumb name. They were hippies, so I guess they were into peculiar names. I've

16

got a brother named Sky. That's even worse, don't you think?" Without waiting for an answer she asked, "What's your name?"

"Samantha Tate. My friends call me Sam."

"My parents said someone named Weirton was moving in," Jazz said. She had her hands on her hips and stared at Sam as though accusing her of being an impostor.

Sam bristled. She didn't really like to explain why her last name was different from her mother's. "That's my stepfather's name," she answered shortly.

The brief explanation seemed to satisfy Jazz. "Are we going to be friends?" she asked bluntly.

Sam was startled. "I guess so," she answered.

"I live in that house over there." Jazz pointed, and Sam noticed the outline of the house nearly hidden by the woods.

"Are these your woods?" Sam asked.

"Nope," Jazz said cheerfully. "They're yours. But that tree is a perfect place to take pictures. See that path? The deer go by here all the time on their way to the river to drink. I've gotten some great pictures here."

"I'd like to see them."

"Come on over to my house. I've got my own darkroom. I'll show you, if you're interested," Jazz said. "Hey, what grade are you in at school?"

"I'm going into the sixth grade," Sam told her. "At home I would have still been in elementary, but here I have to go to the middle school."

"Hey, that's great. I'm going to be in the sixth grade, too. Sky is in the seventh. We can all take the bus together."

Sam's stomach gave a hungry rumble. "I'd better get home right now," she said. "If my parents wake up and don't find me, they might be worried."

"Come over later," Jazz said. "I'll introduce you to my parents. Mom and Dad are into back-to-nature stuff. They're a little weird, but they're pretty nice. You can meet Sky, too. He's the genius of the family." She waved as she started down the path to her house. "Maybe I'll show you my toads, too," she called back cheerfully.

CHAPTER THREE

A YELLOW MOVING van was parked in front of the house, and two men were carrying Mrs. Weirton's old desk inside when Sam returned. Samantha's mother hovered around them, watching anxiously as the men maneuvered the antique piece through the door. "Oh, there you are," Mom said, wiping a smudge from her cheek. "I was getting worried."

"I just was out looking around," Sam said. Her mother waved an arm toward the kitchen. "There's cereal and milk in the kitchen. I've got to show the men where to put everything."

The living room was crowded with boxes. Sam wove her way around them, heading for the kitchen. Julie was already eating. As usual, in spite of the confusion, she looked gorgeous. The hour Sam had spent in the woods was most likely spent by Julie in the bathroom. Sam ran her hands through her own hair. In spite of her good intentions, she never seemed to have time to fix it. She shrugged. Jazz didn't seem the sort to be impressed by perfect hair.

"I met one of the neighbors," Sam told her sister. "She's kind of different, but I think I like her. She said her family is interested in nature. I think she has pet toads."

Julie looked up with interest, but after hearing the last part of the sentence, she rolled her eyes. "Oh, goody," she said with broad sarcasm. "I can hardly wait to meet her."

"She seems really nice, and she'll be in my grade," Sam informed her.

"You're not going to get off to a very good start in middle school by being friends with a weirdo," Julie said.

"She's not weird, just different."

Julie's look said plainly that as far as she was concerned, there was little difference. Sam didn't defend her new friend further. She poured herself a bowlful of sugared cereal and splashed on the milk.

Jim wandered into the kitchen and made himself a cup of instant coffee. "Is that all you're having for breakfast?" he said. Then he laughed. "I guess that's all we stocked in the cupboards." He sat at the table with them. "The movers are just about done." His gray eyes studied Samantha. "Who's not weird?"

"I met the girl next door. She invited me over to look at her toads."

"Maybe they were all handsome princes, and when she kissed them, they turned into toads," Julie said, laughing.

"It sounds like we have interesting neighbors," Jim said. "Aside from toad-keeping neighbors, what do you think of your new home, now that you've seen it in daylight?" He picked up the box of cereal Sam had left on the counter. "I don't know why your mother allows you to eat this junk," he mumbled.

"It's nice. I like the woods. But it's not like home," Sam said, reaching a little defiantly for the cereal to pour another bowlful.

"Homesick already?"

"I guess. I miss hearing the ocean," Sam admitted.

"When I was a kid, my family lived in Chicago. It was a noisy neighborhood. All day long there were

21

kids crying, dogs barking, people arguing, cars honking."

"I thought you always lived here," Julie said.

"Nope. I moved to Ohio when I got my job," Jim answered. He was an engineer for a huge electronics manufacturer in a nearby city. "I've been here for nearly ten years, except for the year the company transferred me to Oregon. I'm glad they did," he added with a smile, "so I could meet my new family."

"I'll bet you were glad to move out of your old neighborhood in Chicago," Julie said.

Jim shook his head. "I missed it. You always miss the town where you were raised."

Mom came into the kitchen and dropped into a chair. "Movers are done," she announced. "Now all we have to do is unpack about a hundred boxes." She smiled weakly. "Promise me we'll never have to move again."

"There are only about twenty boxes," Jim corrected briskly. "And it will go like clockwork if you've labeled everything as I suggested."

"I labeled," Mrs. Weirton said a little testily. "Unfortunately, I don't think the movers could read."

"You just need some organization. I'll distribute the boxes to the right rooms. Julie, you help your mother unpack the kitchen. Samantha, you can do the bathrooms. Then we can all do our own personal things."

"I need to unpack my things now," Julie whined. "I need my curling iron. My hair is a mess."

"You can do that later. No one will see you," Jim said firmly.

Julie's face looked sulky. Jim was being a little bossy, Samantha thought, but his scheme for organization did help. By evening most of the boxes had been unpacked, and the house was beginning to resemble a home.

After dinner Mrs. Weirton and Jim sat together on one end of the couch in the living room. Sam could hear Jim talking softly. Every now and then her mother laughed. They had been grumbling at each other all day, but now it all seemed forgotten.

"It's disgusting," Julie said, suddenly slamming down the plate she was drying. "Mom's in there giggling like some silly kid."

Sam nodded. She knew how Julie felt. It wasn't so much the way her mom was acting as the way it made Sam feel—left out.

"I'll bet she doesn't even think about our real dad anymore," Julie said bitterly.

"I'm sure she remembers him," Sam said, feeling like she should defend her mother. "I thought you liked Jim."

"At first I did. But I didn't know they were going to get so carried away with all this lovey-dovey stuff."

"I think you're supposed to act like that when you get married," Sam said slowly.

"Well, I think they should start acting like grown-ups," Julie said primly.

"They're in love," Sam said, even though she secretly agreed.

"That doesn't mean I have to like it." Julie threw down her towel and stomped out of the kitchen.

Sam quickly wiped off the sinks and hung the dishrag. Her good mood had fled with Julie's angry exit. She decided to walk through the woods to visit Jazz. Stepping into the living room to say she was going out, Sam saw her mother in Jim's arms. Embarrassed, Sam backed out of the room before they saw her.

It was still hot, and the woods were full of the sound of insect songs, punctuated by a woodpecker drilling for a late-night snack. As Sam nervously pushed her way through several tangles of vines, she made up her mind to cut some better walking trails the first time she had a chance. Jazz's house was set back in the woods, and although Sam could see it through the trees, she was hot, sweaty, and itchy by the time she arrived.

A thin, slightly bald man—Jazz's father, Sam

decided—was splitting logs near the edge of the woods. He looked momentarily startled when she appeared, but he quickly recovered, and his face broke into a smile.

"Well, I've seen raccoons and deer come out of the woods, and even an occasional skunk. But this is the first time I've seen a pretty girl. You must be one of the new neighbors . . . unless your name is Goldilocks?"

Sam grinned back at him. "Is Jazz home?"

The back door slammed and Jazz stood on the porch, holding a dish towel. "Don't let him give you a hard time. He teases everyone. Mostly, we just try to ignore him."

"See how badly they treat me," said Mr. McKenna. "We made a mistake when we named her Jazz. Should have called her Sassy."

Sam listened enviously to their easy banter, wondering if she would ever feel that comfortable with Jim. She followed Jazz into the steamy kitchen. "Sorry it's so hot in here. Mom and I have been canning tomatoes," Jazz explained.

It was hot, but Sam thought she rather liked the old-fashioned smell of tomatoes and spices.

A slender young-looking woman brushed a lock of golden brown hair off her face. "You must be Sam. Jazz told me she met you this morning. Welcome to the neighborhood."

"Thanks," Sam answered. Looking at Mrs. McKenna, Sam could see where Jazz got her looks. Mrs. McKenna's eyes sparkled with intelligence and good humor. Her voice was as comfortable as her face.

"You can go visit with Sam," Mrs. McKenna told Jazz. "We're almost done anyway."

Jazz threw down her towel. "Great! Come on, I'll show you around."

The staircase was steep and narrow. Jazz bounded up the stairs two at a time, but at the top, she stopped and waited for Sam. The hallway at the top was almost as wide as a room. A round rag rug set off the gleaming wood floor, and at the far end was a bay window with a built-in seat. There were four doors leading off the hallway. Through the only open one Sam could see pots of dried stems and leaves, and plants hanging upside down from the ceiling. A spicy warm scent spilled from the room.

"This is so nice," Sam exclaimed.

Jazz looked pleased. "I thought you might not like it, since your house is so new. This house was built in eighteen forty-five. Mom and Dad are restoring it. I helped sand these floors," she added proudly.

"What are all those plants?" Sam asked.

"Mom dries them in there. She sells herbs and

potpourri mixes. That's why it smells so nice. This is my room," Jazz said as she reached for the door handle.

Suddenly the door across the hall was flung open. "Have you been in my room again? I'm missing some copper wire." The tall handsome boy with curly brown hair sounded angry.

"I thought you were throwing it away," Jazz said apologetically. "I needed it to fix one of the cages."

"Well, I need it for an experiment. How would you like me to take one of your cages to make a rocket?" the boy snapped. His face flushed a deep red as he noticed Sam for the first time. Hastily he stuffed his shirt into his pants and ran his hand through an unruly mop of dark curls.

There was a minute of tense silence until Jazz chuckled. "This is my brother, Sky. He's the scientist of the family. I guess right now you could call him the mad scientist."

All traces of anger disappeared as Sky looked at his sister and grinned. "I'd rather be a mad scientist than a toad lady," he retorted.

"That's because you don't know how sweet they are," Jazz said.

"Ha! Anybody who thinks toads are sweet is the real crazy person around here."

Sam smiled as she listened to the friendly interchange. Sky McKenna was the most interesting boy she had ever met. Even with a streak of grease across his cheek he was handsome, and when he looked at her with his wide, intelligent eyes, she felt her knees grow suddenly weak. Over his shoulder Sam could see a giant telescope pointed out a window. Instead of a bureau, a long workbench covered with parts lined one wall of his room.

"Sky likes to build rockets," Jazz explained.

"Models?" Sam asked. Her voice sounded strange to her ears.

Sky nodded. "Models, but with real engines. I'd like to design spacecraft when I grow up."

Sam had never found it hard to talk to boys, but then Sky was nothing like any of the boys she had ever met. She wanted to say something witty and clever. She would have settled for something intelligent, but her mind seemed to have suddenly shriveled. She stood embarrassed and tongue-tied for a long moment before Jazz came to her rescue.

"I'm going to show her my zoo," she said, motioning for Sam to follow.

"I guess I'll see you around," Sky called after them.

"You have an interesting family," Sam said, clearing a space on Jazz's bed and trying to sound nonchalant. She looked around the room, in case her face showed how hard her heart was pounding. One wall was completely covered with photos. Most of them were of animals, and even to Sam's inexperienced eye, they looked very good. Just like Sky, Jazz had a long workbench across one wall. But instead of being covered with rocket parts like Sky's, hers was covered with cages. Peering closer, Sam saw most of them were filled with lizards, snakes, toads, mice, and a bird.

"Mom and Dad encourage us to develop our interests," Jazz said. She reached into one of the cages and picked up a small brownish green lizard. "Like him?" she asked, dangling the lizard in front of Sam as though she were testing Sam's reaction. Sam nodded. "He's cute."

If it had been a test, Sam seemed to have passed. Jazz grinned at her. "His name is Ralph." Jazz set Ralph on her arm. He scurried to her shoulder and perched there, giving Sam an unblinking stare. Sam touched Ralph's head, surprised at the dry feel.

Jazz dropped Ralph gently back in his cage. "Dad will only let me keep them for a while," she said, waving her arms at the cages. "He doesn't believe in disturbing nature. Dad used to be a lawyer. But he got tired of the rat race, as he called it, and moved us here. Now he just does odd jobs. He's a pretty good carpenter. Mom writes a column for the newspaper and sells herbs."

"My stepdad is allergic to animals," Sam said. "But we might get a horse. He thinks it might be okay, since it won't be in the house with him. We have to build a barn and put some fencing up first. But maybe in a couple of months."

"That will be nice," Jazz said, sounding less than enthusiastic.

"Don't you like horses?"

"They're all right. I guess I like little critters better. But a lot of the girls at school do. You'll probably get really popular when they find out you have one. There is a riding stable just down the road. A lot of the girls come out on the weekends to ride."

"That sounds like fun."

"Yeah, I guess. Maybe they will ask you to go with them."

Suddenly Sam understood. She shrugged and smiled at her new friend. "They probably won't."

Jazz gave her a piercing look. "What will you do if they do?"

"I don't know," Sam answered honestly. "I think we are going to get horses, but to be honest, I've never ridden. I've never even been around them very much. So I guess I'll have to do a little practicing before I go with anyone else." She was aware that Jazz was waiting for something more in her answer. "I haven't even met those girls yet. Maybe they won't like me. Or maybe I won't like them."

Her answer seemed to satisfy Jazz. "I don't fit in very well," she admitted. "I guess everyone thinks I'm weird because I'm interested in photography and ecology and things like that. I've got better things to do than sit around talking about what someone is wearing. Most of the time I would rather read than talk." She looked at Samantha. "I like talking to you, though."

Sam could not get Sky out of her mind. "Do you have a boyfriend?" she asked.

Jazz shook her head. "Nobody is weird enough to like me."

"I don't either," Sam admitted. "My sister thinks you have to have one in middle school." Sam stretched out on the bed. She felt comfortable with Jazz, as though they had been friends a long time. "Do you ever think about kissing a boy?"

Jazz blushed. "Sometimes. You know what I can't figure out? How do you kiss without your nose getting in the way?"

Sam giggled. "I think you have to tip your head."

"How do you know how to do it the first time? Do you suppose it just comes naturally?"

"We could watch some romantic movies," Samantha said, sitting up again. "We have a VCR.

31

We could put it on 'pause' just as they are about to kiss and study it."

"That's a great idea," Jazz said. "Not that I am likely to need that information anytime soon."

"I think you're pretty," Sam said. "I'll bet you could get a boyfriend if you wanted."

Jazz grinned. "Well, while we're waiting for Prince Charming, let's go see if Mom will give us some cookies. I'm starving."

CHAPTER FOUR

"**I** AM SO nervous, I'm sick," Sam said. She sat on the edge of her bed, clutching her stomach, and groaned. "Maybe I shouldn't go today."

"You know you always get sick when you're excited," Julie said unsympathetically. "It will be worse tomorrow. Then everyone will stare at you when you walk in the class."

"What if I throw up right in front of everyone? Then they'll really stare."

"I'm starting a new school, too, you know." Julie patted the last blond curl in place and stepped away from the mirror.

"Yeah, grade school," Sam said scornfully. "That's not anywhere near as bad as middle school. Besides," she added, softening her insult, "you always look pretty. Just look at me. I look like a broom handle. A broom handle with fat feet . . . and a blotchy face."

Julie looked at her critically. "You don't have fat feet or a blotchy face." She paused. "Now you *do* look a little bit like a broom handle," she teased.

"Urgh," Sam cried in despair. "That's it. I'm not going. I'm just going to go back to bed and stay there until I'm an old woman."

"Come on," Julie sighed in exasperation. "You look fine."

"You don't even look nervous," Sam complained, giving herself a last frown in the mirror. "It's easy for you, but I hate trying to make new friends."

Julie looked pleased as they walked downstairs for breakfast. "Just act mysterious, and people will be dying to meet you. And you look great, too. Just take my advice. Don't hang around Jazz too much. People will figure you are as weird as she is."

"I like her. Besides, she's the only friend I have."

Julie shrugged. "Don't say I didn't warn you. You'll find out when your only friends are the misfits."

Breakfast in their house had always been a rather casual affair, so Sam was surprised to see their mother flipping pieces of French toast. "What's this about misfits?" Mrs. Weirton asked, spatula poised in midair.

"I was just explaining to Sam that middle school is a lot different. You have to be careful how you dress and who you pick for friends," Julie said.

"She thinks I shouldn't be friends with Jazz," Sam said.

"Do you like Jazz?" asked Jim. Seeing him at the table made Sam realize why the change in her mother's morning routine. Jim believed in the importance of a good breakfast. That was one change for the better, Sam thought, as her mother placed a golden stack of French toast and crisp bacon strips in front of her.

Sam reached for the syrup bottle. "I like her a lot," she said.

"Then you should be friends with her. Sounds pretty simple to me."

Julie sighed. "Maybe it was that way when you went to school. Nowadays it's different. Your whole career at school could depend on first impressions."

"Sounds to me like it's all the more important to just be yourself," Mom said. "It would be awfully hard to maintain a false image for seven more years."

Julie gave Sam a conspiratorial look and rolled

her eyes. But Sam was confused. She knew Mom and Jim were probably right. But Jazz was a little weird. It would be terrible to go to school for seven more years as a social outcast.

"I had a weird friend when I was in school," Jim said. "The teachers weren't too fond of him because he sat in the back of the room and made animal noises. Sounded like you were in a jungle. I liked him, though. He could belch on demand ten times in a row."

"I suppose he became a comedian or something?" Julie asked, sounding half-interested.

Jim smiled ruefully. "Real life's not that perfect. I think he works in a factory in Akron."

"So what's the point of the story?" Julie asked impatiently.

"Nothing. I just thought you might like to hear it," Jim said.

Julie frowned. "It was a dumb story."

Sam looked from Julie to Jim, surprised at the tension in the air between them.

"Have you girls made your beds?" Jim asked.

"Mom always lets us wait until after school," Julie said.

"Your mom was working and in a big rush to leave. You have time enough to do it before school now."

"Mine's made," Sam offered.

"Of course," Julie almost snarled. "Little Miss Perfect."

"That's enough," Jim said. "Go back up and make yours."

"You are not my boss," Julie shouted, jumping up and almost knocking over her chair.

"I am," Mom said quietly. "Do as Jim says. Go up and make your bed."

Julie stomped all the way upstairs and slammed her door shut. Sam looked at Jim, feeling as if she should apologize for her sister. Before Jim and Mom had married, Julie had been thrilled about the idea, but now she seemed to resent everything Jim said.

"It takes time to adjust," Mom said to no one in particular.

"Did you check everything on the list of school supplies I made for you?" Jim asked Sam.

Sam nodded and gestured to her backpack. "It's all in there. Julie has all her stuff, too," she added quickly, trying to avoid another conflict.

"Are you sure you don't want us to go with you the first day?" Jim asked.

"Yes," said Sam. In truth, she wanted nothing more. "It would look dumb. I *am* in the sixth grade now."

A few minutes later, sitting on the noisy bus with Jazz, Sam wished she could take back her brave words. Almost everyone seemed to know one another, and the bus rang with happy shouts of greeting after the long summer. Groups of twos and threes fell into conversation. A few kids gave Sam a curious stare, but most simply ignored her.

Sam twisted in her seat to look at Julie sitting several rows behind. She was already talking to the girl sitting next to her. By the time the bus stopped at the grade school, they appeared to be old friends.

"At least you've got me," Jazz said perceptively.

Sam glanced at her new friend. Judging by Jazz's clothes, Sam could not have guessed it was the first day of school. Her own clothes felt stiff and new, but Jazz was wearing an old pair of jeans with a slightly unraveled hem and a T-shirt emblazoned with the words "Save the Jungle."

"Do you have your schedule yet?" Jazz held up hers, but Sam shook her head.

"There wasn't time to send it to me. I have to go to the office."

"We can sit together at lunch even if we don't have the same homeroom." Jazz tucked her schedule back in her pocket.

"That would be great," Sam said. There was nothing worse than sitting by yourself at lunchtime. No matter how much you tried to pretend it was by choice, everyone knew. But even more awful would be to sit at a table already taken by a group of friends without being asked. Sam twisted around in her seat again. "Don't you know anybody on the bus?"

Jazz shrugged. "A few. I had a really good friend last year. But her mother and father were missionary doctors. They went to Africa to help with a drought. She wrote me a letter and said it was really awful. Children were dying from hunger every day."

Worrying about making friends seemed insignificant next to starving babies. Sam settled down in her seat and tried to look comfortable. But as the bus maneuvered into the parking lot in front of the school, her stomach gave an unhappy lurch.

Washington Middle School was a grim brick building, four stories high. Hundreds of windows stared an unfriendly welcome.

"It looks like a prison," Jazz observed cheerfully. "Come on. I'll go to the office with you."

Jazz looked dismayed when they saw the large crowd milling about the office. She glanced at her watch. "You'd probably end up being late," Sam told her. "I'll see you at lunch, or maybe before, if we're lucky." She crossed her fingers for luck.

"I'd better go hunt up my room. It's 302, so I suppose the third floor would be a good place to start the search." Jazz waved and headed for the stairs.

Sam squeezed her way through the crowd and waited silently until at last she reached the counter.

"What's your problem?" The woman behind the counter looked frazzled and weary even though it was only quarter to eight in the morning. The woman tapped her pencil impatiently. "No changing schedules today."

Quickly Sam explained that she was new. "I think Mom called in a couple of days ago."

The woman rummaged in a file and pulled out a card. "Room 310. Mrs. Spritz," she said shortly.

"Where—" Sam started to say, but the secretary motioned to a girl standing nearby. "Heather, you are in 310. Take this new girl up with you," she called loudly.

Sam cringed at the room full of curious eyes as she stumbled out after Heather. The hallways were a little less crowded because nearly everyone had found their rooms by now. Heather gave her a sideways look. "Where are you from?"

"Oregon," Sam said. "We just moved here last week."

"Is that what the kids wear to school in Oregon?" Heather asked.

Heather's voice was carefully neutral, as though

she was asking a friendly question. But there was a mocking look in her eyes that made Sam hesitate with her answer.

Sam's jeans were new but faded to a soft blue, and Mrs. Weirton had let her splurge on the turquoise pullover that brought out the color in her eyes. Sam had felt rather pleased with her outfit, standing in front of the mirror at home. But now, seeing the challenge in Heather's eyes, she was not so sure. Her clothes didn't seem much different from those worn by the girls she had passed in the hall. Heather herself was dressed in a similar fashion except for some highly advertised labels.

"Is there something wrong with my clothes?" Sam asked, trying to hide her dismay.

"Oh, no," Heather said smoothly. "Those were probably great in Oregon, but here the styles are different." She gave Sam another sideways glance. "I'm sure it would be the same if I moved to Oregon," she added generously. "I'd probably dress wrong. You know, too stylish." She went on chatting comfortably as though unaware of the effect her words were having on Sam. "Some of us belong to a club. As a matter of fact, I'm the president. We discuss what kind of clothes we should wear and other things like that. Maybe later we might let you join. We'd want to watch you for a while first, of course. To see if you'd fit in." She

41

pointed to the label on her jeans. "I wouldn't be caught dead in any other brand."

Several girls waved at Heather and stared curiously at Sam. Heather ran off to greet them, leaving Sam standing alone in the hall. The girls pulled out their schedules and compared classroom assignments. Heather gave an exuberant squeal when she discovered two of the girls would have the same homeroom teacher as she did. Sam waited awkwardly, forgotten for the moment. Something was said in a low voice, and there were barely suppressed giggles as the girls looked her way. Sam glanced at the clock. In another minute the bell would ring, and she would be forced into walking in late.

"Maybe I should go ahead and try to find the room," she said, walking toward them.

Heather looked up and nodded. She made no attempt to introduce her to the other girls. "It's just up the stairs," she said, dismissing her. "You'll find it."

Face burning, Sam took the stairs two at a time and barely squeezed in the room before the bell rang. Heather and her friends slid in a second later and grabbed seats together at the back of the room.

The rest of the morning was a haze of listening to rules, passing out textbooks, filling in forms, and getting assigned lockers. Mrs. Spritz, the homeroom teacher, was tall and reedy, with a high fluty voice that seemed out of character with her businesslike manner. Sam thought she might like the woman, although she did seem rather strict.

Mrs. Spritz had not commented on the late arrival of Heather and her friends, but during the roll call she gave them a pointed look. "You will be in your seats, ready for work, when the bell rings. No exceptions. If you are not, you will go to the office and explain why."

"I apologize for being late, Mrs. Spritz," Heather said sweetly. "The office secretary asked me to show that new girl to the room."

Sam looked at Heather in disbelief. She was making it sound as though Sam had caused her to be late. But Heather avoided her gaze and smiled serenely at the teacher. Mrs. Spritz, however, did not seem impressed. "If that happens again, I am sure the office will be glad to give you a note," she said dryly before she went on to explain the other class rules.

The sixth grade did not change classes as often as the seventh and eighth grades. Except for gym, industrial arts, and science, Sam's class would stay in the same room. Sam listened with relief. It was going to be hard enough to adjust to this crowded school full of unfamiliar faces without

43

having to search for different rooms. A wave of homesickness swept over her as she remembered her old school. It had been much smaller. Not everyone had been a friend, but at least she had known them. Here, it wasn't so much that everyone was unfriendly, it was more that they looked right through her as though she were invisible or didn't exist.

By lunchtime she was starving. She hurried to the cafeteria, still longing for a friendly face. To her relief she spotted Jazz as soon as she walked in the door.

"How'd it go?" Jazz asked, giving her a shrewd look.

"Awful," Sam admitted. "The only girl who spoke to me was a snob."

"Give it time," Jazz advised. "There are actually lots of nice kids here."

Sam noted that Jazz did not seem to be Miss Popularity either, although several people stopped to say hello. Then she chided herself for unkind thoughts. Jazz had not only offered friendship, she had offered it unconditionally. It was hard to imagine Jazz waiting to see if someone wore the right clothes before becoming friends.

"Want a bite of bean sprouts?" Jazz offered.

Sam peeked into the container. It looked like a wriggling mass of stems. "No, thanks," she said quickly, reaching into her own bag for a bologna sandwich.

"You wouldn't eat that if you knew what was in it," Jazz said calmly. "They just grind up all the garbage that's left after they butcher. My family doesn't eat meat at all, but even if we did, I'd never eat that."

Sam took a bite and swallowed hard. Somehow it didn't taste as good as usual.

"I like meat," she said, to get even. "There's nothing better than a good steak with lots of red juice dripping out of it."

Jazz looked a little sick. "Vampire," she said, grinning at Sam.

Sam grinned back. "How do you know all those vegetables you're eating aren't really alive? Maybe you just can't hear them. Maybe when you cut off a head of cabbage, it's really screaming. And corn on the cob. Maybe every time you take a bite, it's yelling, 'Ow, ow, ow.' "

Jazz laughed just as she took a drink, spraying orange juice over both of them. This sent them into gales of laughter, until Heather and her friends strolled by with a disdainful glance in their direction.

"Honestly. Some people are so immature," Heather said loud enough for Sam to hear. "You would think they were still in elementary school."

"What's so funny?" Sky appeared suddenly and slid into the seat next to Sam. Immediately her mind went blank, and her tongue tied itself in knots.

Heather's reaction was completely different. "Hello, Sky," Heather purred, suddenly all smiles. She looked at Sky and then at Sam. "Are you two friends?"

"We're neighbors," Sky said shortly.

"Oh, isn't that nice," Heather said smoothly. She turned to Jazz with a bright smile. "Do you still collect toads? Or is it snakes?"

"Both," Jazz said. "But I don't collect them. I study them so I can take pictures."

"You don't have to be so grouchy. I was just interested." Heather took on a look of hurt innocence.

"I'll bring a couple of snakes to your house," Jazz said wickedly, "since you're so interested."

"I'm into bigger animals. Like horses," Heather said. "Do you know how to ride?" she asked Sam.

"We might get some horses," Sam said. "As soon as Jim, my stepfather, can get a barn built."

Heather looked at her with added interest. "Maybe I'll come over and visit when you do." She flipped her hair back and leaned toward Sky. "Will you be there?"

"Horses are too slow. I like rockets," Sky said.

He stood up and crumpled his lunch bag. "I have to go," he told Jazz. "I just stopped to tell you I'm staying after school. For science club. Tell Mom when you get home."

Heather looked disappointed. But she covered it quickly and walked away with her friends without even a good-bye.

"That's the bunch I told you about," Jazz said, looking after them.

"Well, I don't have to worry about their asking me to join," Sam said.

"No loss on your part," Jazz said. She gave Sam another of her knowing looks. "Or is it?"

"Of course not," Sam said hotly. "They're just a bunch of snobs." Nevertheless, she couldn't help being a little irritated at Jazz. It would have helped if her one friend could have introduced her to people. But Jazz didn't seem the least bit concerned with belonging to a group. If she didn't make such an effort to be different, maybe she would have more friends.

CHAPTER FIVE

MRS. SPRITZ leaned on her elbows
and looked at the class. "I like projects," she said
in her musical voice. "It's fine to learn the lessons
in the book, but projects sort of bring it all together. That way you get a chance to use what you
are learning, and I can see how many of your lessons have soaked into your brain."

From the back of the class came the quiet
sound of water dripping, and Samantha choked
back a giggle. After several weeks in class she
knew it was Steven Gorden. He had already been
scolded several times. He was the only one in the
room who had not had difficulty changing decimals into fractions. But he could not seem to sit

still for more than five minutes without getting into trouble. *Drip!* It sounded exactly like water dripping into a puddle.

Mrs. Spritz ignored the noise, but a ghost of a smile crossed her face. "Most of the time I will assign you personal projects, but for this first project I'll have you work in teams."

Drip!

Mrs. Spritz tapped her pencil eraser on the desk. "Steven, I certainly hope that sound does not represent all the knowledge I've worked so hard to put in your head, leaking out."

An echoing drip sounded from another corner of the room. Mrs. Spritz's usually amiable look was replaced with a stern one. "Class, you may have noticed by now that when I am upset, I tap my pencil on my desk. Like so," she said, demonstrating. "Now this silly habit is one that I used to try to correct, but no longer. Does anyone want to venture a guess why?"

Mary Frances raised her hand. She was a brisk, no-nonsense girl who had been nicknamed "Brain." Sam thought she might like to be friends with her, but Mary Frances seldom spoke to anyone except Keikoa, a shy pretty girl who was also an *A* student. "It's a signal to us that we had better straighten up?"

Mrs. Spritz looked pleased. "Wonderful. That's

exactly right. Perhaps we should practice. Steven, stand up and make your leaky-faucet imitation. Anyone else who wants to join him may do so."

Looking embarrassed but obviously enjoying himself, Steven puckered his mouth and snapped the outside of his cheek with his thumb and forefinger. He was accompanied by a loud chorus of drips interspersed with several jungle-bird calls. The orchestra continued for several more seconds until Mrs. Spritz tapped her pencil on the desk. Immediately a silence fell over the room.

"Ahh." Mrs. Spritz beamed at them. "I knew this was a brilliant class. Now let's try it one more time so there is no mistake. Noise, please!" *Tap, tap.*

After the second demonstration, Mrs. Spritz went on to explain the project. "Every year our school has a World Culture Day. Each team will prepare a display for its favorite country. You can have maps, reports, pictures. If you want to go all out, perhaps a sample of the country's food. You will also be expected to give a two- or three-minute talk about the country you've chosen."

Holding her hand up to silence the loud groans, Mrs. Spritz continued. "In the interest of fairness, I have devised a plan to divide into groups. I have divided the class into thirds and placed two-thirds of your names in a sack. When I call the rest of your names, you will come up and draw two names out of the sack. The three of you will be a group."

Sam crossed her fingers for luck. Maybe this would be a chance to make new friends. At least the others in her group would have to talk to her. She held her breath as each name was called.

Steven reached into the sack. "And the winners are . . . Heather Collins and Samantha Tate!"

"You may take a few minutes to meet with your group and decide on your country," Mrs. Spritz said before Sam could absorb her bad luck. Heather frowned. She leaned over and whispered something to Kirsten, and both girls turned and stared at Sam. With a sinking feeling in the pit of her stomach, Sam walked over to Heather's desk.

Heather waved her hand. "Mrs. Spritz, could we do a project by ourselves if we want?" she asked loudly.

Sam felt her ears burning. She wished a black hole would open in the middle of Room 310 and suck her in.

"Do you get the feeling we're not wanted?" Steven whispered in Sam's ear.

"The groups are set," said Mrs. Spritz. "If you would like to do an extra project by yourself, you may."

"Well, what country do you not want to do with us?" Steven asked Heather.

"I just wanted to make sure I got an *A* on the project," Heather said, still looking sulky.

"I want an *A*, too," Sam said.

"I'm not very good at reports. But I'm pretty good at art," Steven said helpfully. "I could make all the maps and things."

Heather shrugged. "So what country shall we do?"

"How about China?" Sam suggested. "It's an interesting country and probably not too many others will choose it."

"I'd rather do Mexico," Heather said. "My parents went to Acapulco last year. They brought back a lot of jewelry and pottery. I think they would let me use some for a display. Besides, we could fix tacos for everyone to taste."

Reluctantly, Sam nodded. "I guess so. I don't have anything from China."

Both girls looked at Steven, who grinned cheerfully back. "It doesn't matter to me. I can draw Mexico just as easily as China."

"We'd better do some research at the library," Sam suggested.

"I have stuff to do after school," Heather said. "But I could meet you there Saturday. Would about one o'clock be okay?"

Sam nodded. Maybe after they had worked together Heather would be more friendly. "I'll be there," she promised just as the bell rang.

After school Sam rummaged in her closet, looking for something special to wear to the library. There was a small restaurant next door to the library. Maybe Heather would go there with her, and Sam could buy her a Coke.

She was feeling almost happy when she went downstairs. Julie was watching TV in the living room. Sam picked up her science book and started to skim over her homework. But as soon as Jim walked in the door, there was trouble.

"Who left the curling iron plugged in this morning?" Jim scolded.

"I guess I did," Julie said nonchalantly.

"Are you trying to set the house on fire?"

"I just forgot," Julie snapped. "You don't have to make such a big deal out of it."

"A house burning down is a rather big deal to me," Jim said. "If you do it again, I'll put the curling iron away for good."

"I have to have it for my hair," Julie said.

"Then don't forget it again," Jim said with a look that meant business.

"I'm getting sick and tired of his bossing us around," Julie fumed when Jim left the room.

"It is dangerous to leave it plugged in," Sam

said. "You know Mom's scolded you for leaving it on, too."

"Oh, sure, take his side," Julie sneered. "A few months ago you were doing anything you could think of to get rid of him. Now you act like he's Mr. Wonderful."

Sam blushed, remembering. "But now he and Mom are married. We should give him a chance."

Julie made an ugly face and stuck out her tongue. She turned up the volume on the television so it was too loud for conversation. A minute later Jim walked back in the room and snapped off the set.

"I had to bring some work home from the office," he said grimly. "And I think you can see your sister is doing homework. One thing I insist on in a home is common courtesy."

There was an uncomfortable silence when Jim stormed back to the small room across the hall that he'd set up as an office. Sam left the room and went to look for her mother. She found her in the kitchen, putting frosting on a cake and humming softly. She looked up and smiled when Sam entered the room.

"Want to lick the beaters?" she asked.

"I'm too old for that," Sam declared. Neverthe-less, she took a beater and ran her tongue over the frosting. "Umm, pretty good. You're kind of enjoying being a homebody, aren't you?"

"I guess I am," Mrs. Weirton admitted. "It's kind of nice to do all the things I never had time for when I was working."

"Don't you miss it?"

"Miss what? Working?"

"Well, that. But mostly getting out and having friends."

Her mother shook her head. "Not yet. I'm enjoying my family. And I am making friends with Jazz's mother. I'm also thinking about volunteering at the hospital, so I would meet a few people that way."

"Do grown-ups talk to one another? I mean when they are strangers."

Mrs. Weirton sat down at the table and patted the chair next to her for Sam to sit. "Still haven't made friends with anyone but Jazz?"

"It's not that the kids are mean," Sam said. "It's just that they all know one another. About all they speak to me for is to ask me to pass a note. But Heather is one of the most popular girls in the school. If she liked me, maybe I could make some friends."

"Some people might think it fortunate to have one good friend," Mrs. Weirton said thoughtfully.

"I'm not sure Heather is the kind of girl you want to make friends with, from what you've told me about her. You've only been in school a couple of weeks. Perhaps you're rushing things. Give the other kids time to know you. Do you speak to them?"

"Oh, sure. I run up to them and say, 'Hi. I'm Samantha Tate. Do you want to be friends?'" Sam's voice had a bitter edge.

"Maybe you should join some after-school activities."

"Like what? I'm not good at anything." Sam put the beater in the sink and shrugged.

"How do you know? You haven't tried everything."

"I always feel so dumb when I try something new. Especially in front of people." Sam tried to make her mother understand.

"They had to learn, too."

"Things like that don't seem to bother other people," Sam said.

"Sure it does. They just don't let it show," Mrs. Weirton said firmly. "Maybe you could try out for a sport," she suggested.

Sam shrugged. "I don't really like sports very much. Jazz is trying to get me to join the photography club. But I'm not sure I want to do that either."

"There must be something you'd like to do," Mrs. Weirton said.

"Some of the girls have a riding club," Sam volunteered.

"That sounds like fun. Maybe they'll ask you to join when they know you better."

Sam shrugged. "Heather is one of them. A couple of the other girls seem all right."

Mrs. Weirton patted her arm. "I wish I could help you more. But I still think the others will be friendlier when they know you better."

"I suppose," Sam said a little doubtfully.

Sam helped her mother dish out dinner. Mrs. Weirton had splurged with steaks and her special scalloped potatoes, everyone's favorite. For a few minutes the family ate in companionable silence, enjoying the meal.

"Terrific dinner," Jim said, pushing back his plate.

"Lauren is having a birthday sleep-over party," Julie announced suddenly. "It's sort of an early-Halloween/birthday party."

"Who's Lauren?" asked Mrs. Weirton.

Julie shrugged. "Just a girl at school."

"I don't know about the sleep-over," Mom said. "We don't know her parents at all."

"Everyone else is going," Julie said. "I'll bet their parents don't all know Lauren's parents."

"We haven't even met Lauren," Jim said.

"I'm not a baby," Julie shouted. "I can pick out my own friends."

"True." Jim nodded. "But if we don't know anything about them, you don't spend the night."

"Why are you always so mean?" Julie yelled. "I wish Mom had never met you."

The words hung over the room like a black cloud. Sam sighed. For once she sided with Julie. It wasn't their fault they hadn't lived there long enough to know everyone. Julie shoved back her chair and raced from the room. A second later they heard the door to her bedroom slam shut. Her mother and Jim exchanged a worried look. Sam felt left out, forgotten, standing in the middle of someone else's war.

"We need a family project," she blurted out. She hadn't even thought before she said it, but now that she had, she realized it was a good idea.

Jim gave her a crooked smile. "You're very perceptive. Any suggestions?"

She wanted to remind them that they were the parents, and it was their job, not hers, but she shook her head and shrugged.

"We could make a list of ideas," Jim said thoughtfully.

Another list. It was Jim's answer to everything. He would probably make a list of things to do before he died. Sighing, Sam got up and started to clear the plates.

Jim shook his head. "It's Julie's turn to do the dishes."

"I don't mind," Sam said, but her mother had already started upstairs after her sister. Suddenly Sam wanted to be away from all of them. She grabbed her jacket and ducked out the back door.

CHAPTER SIX

MOST OF the leaves were already tinged with color, making the woods glow in the early evening light. The trail was littered with hickory nuts and black walnuts, food for the squirrels and other small animals that shared the land. A chipmunk skittered in front of her, then stopped a few feet away. Head cocked comically to one side, it watched her. Sam wished she had brought her camera. Then she laughed at herself. She was starting to think like Jazz. Even though Sam wasn't interested enough to join the photography club, Jazz had been giving her a lot of tips about taking good pictures.

"Hello," called Mr. McKenna. "Is it Goldilocks or Little Red Riding Hood?"

"The big, bad wolf," Sam joked back.

Mr. McKenna put a bunch of brush on the pile he was making.

"Do I detect some sarcasm?"

"Why does life have to be so complicated?" Sam said, throwing herself down on a log.

"Whew," said Mr. McKenna. "Why don't you at least give me an easier question, like explaining the universe."

Sam grinned. She could always count on Mr. McKenna to cheer her up.

"Want to talk about it?"

"I don't know," Sam answered. "It's just that Julie and Jim are fighting again. Sometimes I don't know whose side I'm on."

"That's the price we pay for growing up, I guess," Mr. McKenna said.

"Fighting?"

"No. I mean being able to see other people's points of view. A child only thinks about what he wants. But as you grow older, you begin to see that most of the time there isn't really a black-and-white answer. Jim is trying hard to be a dad. He expects you girls to be happy about that and act like he thinks you should. Julie is growing up, trying to stretch for a little independence. Maybe she really wants Jim to be a dad, but she's lost one dad already. Maybe she's afraid she'll be hurt again. Your mother's caught in the middle. And you, where do you fit?"

"Out in the cold," Sam said with a sigh. "Most of the time I just stay in my room so I don't have to listen to them."

Mr. McKenna gave her the same look she had seen so often in Jazz.

Sam stared out at the woods. "I've been so unhappy at school, I guess I haven't helped very much at home."

"It takes time to fit in after you move. And it takes a lot of hard work to make a family. More than that, it takes a lot of love to cement it together. Give it some time," Mr. McKenna said wisely.

Time. Mr. McKenna and her mother must be on the same wavelength. It was easy for them to talk. Neither of them had spent the whole day at school being ignored by everyone except Jazz. Sam stood up and brushed off her pants. "I guess I'll go talk to Jazz."

"She's out in the barn, making a bird feeder," Mr. McKenna said, waving good-bye.

Jazz was sanding the edges of the wooden feeder when Sam walked in the barn.

"What do you think of it?" she asked, looking up and smiling.

"It's great," Sam said, admiring it. "Did you make it by yourself?"

When Jazz nodded, Sam laughed ruefully. "Last year in school I had to take wood shop. It was a disaster."

"I like to work with wood," Jazz said, running her hands over the birdhouse, checking for rough spots. "Want to help me paint it?"

For a few minutes the girls painted in companionable silence. They were standing back, admiring the finished job, when Sky entered the barn.

"I met Mister Rogers today," Sky said. "He said, 'Won't you be my neighbor?' But I said, 'No, thank you. Samantha Tate is already my neighbor.' "

In spite of, or perhaps because of, her nervousness, Sam was seized with a fit of giggles. She laughed so hard, it made her eyes water.

"Hey," Sky protested. "I know I'm funny, but not *that* funny."

Jazz was laughing now, too. "Maybe you're looking at the wrong career, Sky. Maybe you should be a comic."

"Maybe I should be one of those guys who wears a paper bag over his head: rocket scientist by day, comic by night. . . . What do you give a sick alligator?" Sky asked.

Sam shook her head, her laughter almost under control.

"Gatorade," Sky said.

Both girls stopped laughing. "That's the worst joke I ever heard," Jazz said.

"Me, too," Sam said, once again overtaken by uncontrollable giggles.

Sky shook his head. "Women!" he said in mock disgust. "I don't have to stand here and be insulted. I really just came out to see if you two would like to play a game of Scrabble with me. Then you can see where my skill really lies."

"Ha! I beat him every time," Jazz said to Sam. "Come on. It should only take the two of us about ten minutes to wipe him out."

Sky went ahead to set up the game while Sam helped Jazz put away the paint and brushes.

"It's nice that you and Sky get along so well," Sam said as they trudged into the house.

"That's because I let her win now and then," said Sky, overhearing them.

Jazz threw a couch pillow at her brother. "After she sees you play, she'll know that's a laugh."

But the games ended in a draw, with each person winning one. "We'd better play one more game to determine the champion," Sky said.

"Oh, gosh," Sam said, looking at the clock. "I didn't know it was so late. It's completely dark," she added, thinking of the walk back through the woods.

"I'll get a flashlight, and we'll walk with you," Sky offered.

"Thanks." Sam smiled at him. It was hard to be shy with someone you had just beaten at Scrabble.

"Will your parents be upset?" Jazz asked as they hurried over the trail.

"They probably haven't noticed I'm gone," Sam said. "They were arguing with Julie when I left."

When they reached her yard, Sam waved goodbye. She watched the flashlight bobbing along back through the woods for a minute before she reluctantly opened the door and slipped in.

Jim was sitting alone at the kitchen table. His smile did not erase the melancholy look on his face.

"I'm sorry I'm late. We started playing Scrabble, and I didn't realize what time it was."

Jim nodded. Sam walked past, heading for her room. "Where's Mom? I need some help with my math."

"You may not be aware of this," Jim said bleakly, "but I, too, finished school. In fact, I attended several math classes while I was there."

"I—I guess I never thought of asking you," Sam said. "Would you?"

"I'd be delighted," Jim said, looking a little brighter. "What are you doing?"

"Changing decimals into fractions," Sam answered glumly, showing him her half-finished homework paper. Jim studied it intently for a few minutes. "You're making this harder than it is. Let me show you."

After a few minutes Sam looked up from the paper and smiled. "I think I've got it. You're a pretty good teacher, Jim."

Jim grinned at her, looking more like his usual self. "You're a pretty good student."

Julie's door was open a crack when Sam went upstairs. She stuck her head in the room. "Hi."

Julie was combing her hair. Their eyes met in the mirror, and Sam could see from the redness that Julie had been crying. "Did you have a fight with Mom?" Sam asked.

"It's all Jim's fault," Julie burst out. "I hate him."

"I don't think you're giving him a chance," Sam said. "He's really trying."

"I wish he would stop trying and leave me alone." Julie slammed the brush on the dresser and sat there with her shoulders slumped, looking miserable. Sam picked up the brush and ran it down her sister's hair.

"Do you know what I wish?" she asked. Without

waiting, she answered her own question. "I wish we could sit and talk like we used to."

Julie shrugged. "About what?"

"Just about things that are happening. Sky walked me home through the woods tonight. Jazz was with us, but it was his idea."

Julie twisted around. "You like him?"

"I usually get so nervous when he's around. But tonight it was just like we were old friends. We played games and joked. It was great."

"He *is* pretty cute."

"Do you have a boyfriend?"

"There are a couple of boys I like, but I wouldn't exactly call them boyfriends."

"It's getting late, girls. You'd better get ready for bed," called Mrs. Weirton.

"Want me to fix your hair in the morning?" Julie asked as Sam got up reluctantly to leave.

"That would be great," Sam said. Julie had a talent for fixing hair, one that Sam did not share. On an impulse she reached over and gave her sister a quick hug.

Julie looked embarrassed. "Why'd you do that?"

"It's an awful job, but somebody's got to do it," Sam teased. And leaving Julie staring after her in bewilderment, she slipped out the door.

CHAPTER SEVEN

O N SATURDAY afternoon Mrs. Weirton dropped Sam off at the library. "I'll pick you up at four o'clock," she said.

"Thanks, Mom," Sam said, tugging at her new sweater to straighten it. She had dressed carefully, hoping Heather would notice. Her jeans were the latest style, and the rather expensive running shoes she had talked her mother into buying were the popular brand. She had been so excited about getting them that morning that she hadn't paid enough attention to fit. They were already rubbing a little raw spot on her foot. But she tried not to limp as she walked to the library door.

Inside the door she stopped and looked around

for Heather. The library was small but filled with quiet little nooks for studying and reading. She made a quick tour before deciding that Heather had not yet arrived. She picked out a private table and laid out her supplies of paper and pencils. By one-twenty Heather was still not there. Sam looked through all the books on Mexico and brought the ones that looked the best to the table.

She worked steadily, pausing now and then to look up at the clock. At a quarter to two Steven walked through the door. He looked uncomfortable, but when he saw her, he grinned. Sam's heart sank. She knew Heather would not be happy to see Steven.

Still grinning, Steven started toward her, but his foot missed the step in front of the door, and he nearly went sprawling. He managed to stop his forward tumble by grabbing the nearest table, which unfortunately was occupied by a rather scholarly-looking man busily jotting notes from a large stack of papers and books. Just as Steven's hand reached for the table, the man looked up with alarm and scooped up as many papers as he could. But it was too late. Steven grabbed one corner of the table, throwing it out of balance. Books, papers, table, and Steven all fell in a heap with a loud crash.

For a second the library was deathly quiet. Then

everyone moved at once. The librarian scurried over and peered at Steven, who was still collapsed on the floor where he had fallen. "Are you all right?"

Steven sat up, his face burning red. He rubbed at his knee. "I always like to make a grand entrance," he said, laughing sheepishly. He started to pick up some of the man's papers.

"Don't touch those," the man snapped. "I don't know why hooligans like you are allowed in the library."

"But it was an accident," Sam said indignantly.

The librarian stood the table back in place. "It's all right," she told Steven. "I've tripped over that step myself." She spoke soothingly to the man, who was still muttering as he picked up all his papers and books.

"At least the librarian's nice," Steven commented as he followed Sam back to her table. "I've never been in a library before. Except for the one at school, of course."

He sat across from her and wrapped his long legs around the chair. "I didn't used to be so clumsy," he said apologetically. "I guess my legs are getting too long."

Sam smiled. "That's probably the most excitement this library has seen in years. What are you doing here anyway?"

"I heard Heather tell you to meet her here. I thought I should get some ideas for the pictures and stuff. . . ." His voice trailed off as though he expected her to tell him to leave.

"Good idea," Sam said. She pushed several books over to his side of the table. Steven studied them intently for several minutes. "Do you have any paper?" he asked.

Sam pulled several sheets from her notebook, handed them over, and went back to her reading. Steven cleared his throat loudly. "Do you have an extra pencil?"

Sam handed him the pencil and looked at the clock. Two o'clock. It was obvious Heather wasn't coming. Sam tried to tell herself Heather had forgotten. Heather had said she was very busy.

Sam went to the checkout desk. The man was back at his work. He scowled when Sam walked past, but the librarian smiled and pointed to the phone on the desk when Sam asked to make a call.

She was almost ready to hang up when Heather's mother answered the phone. She sounded surprised when Sam explained. "Heather didn't mention the library, dear. Are you sure you're not mistaken about the time? Heather always has her riding lesson at one o'clock on Saturdays."

"I—I guess I misunderstood," Sam stammered. She said good-bye and returned to the table, feeling a little sick.

Steven looked up from his work. "She's not coming," he said. It was more of a statement than a question.

Suddenly Sam understood. "You knew she wasn't coming."

"Heather's locker is next to mine. I heard her telling Kirsten that she was going to a riding lesson. So I thought you might like a little company."

Angry tears burned in Sam's eyes. She brushed them away, hoping Steven hadn't noticed.

Steven turned his sketch toward Sam. "It's not about Mexico, but I could have you eating a taco or something."

Sam gasped. "It's me!"

He had drawn her sitting at the library table, a little frown of concentration on her face as she read from a large book. With only a few pencil strokes, he had captured her on paper.

"You are really good," Sam said. She looked at him in a new light. There was something awkward and coltish about him, as though he didn't quite fit in his body. But his face was open and friendly.

"It was nice of you to come and keep me company," Sam said.

Steven shrugged. "I really did need to get some ideas for pictures."

"How about Aztecs?" Sam said. "They built this really great civilization, but they were terribly bloodthirsty. They skinned people alive and sacrificed people by cutting their hearts out."

"Their main city used to be where Mexico City is now," Steven surprised her by saying. "Only then it was an island with all these causeways going across the water. They filled it all in to make the modern city. That might make one good picture."

"How did you know that?" Sam asked.

Steven shrugged again. "I'm kind of interested in archaeology."

"I didn't know that I was," Sam admitted, "but this is really fascinating. I'll bet we can make a great report. We don't even need Heather."

They worked together until four o'clock, planning out the report and taking notes. By the time Sam's mother arrived to pick her up, she had almost forgotten about Heather.

Her mother raised an eyebrow when she saw Sam saying good-bye to Steven. "I thought you were meeting a girl named Heather."

"So did I," Sam said, explaining about Heather's standing her up.

"That's a pretty dirty trick," Mom said.

"Well, I did have time to do a lot of research," Sam said ruefully. "This will make a great report. And I think I made another friend."

They had only been home a few minutes when a truck turned into the driveway. "I wonder what that is," Sam said. She leaned on the windowsill so she could see.

"It's all the materials for the barn," Mrs. Weirton replied. "The construction company says the workers can start building on Monday."

Julie came out of her room just in time to hear. She stood beside Sam and peeked out. "You mean we're really going to get a horse?"

"Don't get excited yet. It will be a while," Mrs. Weirton said. "After the barn is finished, we will put up a fence." She squeezed in between them and put an arm around each daughter. "Then we'll start looking at horses."

"What if we don't like the same horse?" Sam questioned.

"Jim and I have already talked about that," Mom explained. "I'm sure riding a horse is a lot more fun with company. So we've been talking about two horses, so you can ride together."

"I can't believe it." Julie almost glowed with happiness. "I thought Jim was just talking. I never dreamed he would really do it."

Mrs. Weirton brushed back a strand of hair

from Julie's eyes. "Jim wants you to be happy. He really loves you."

Julie ran off to call all her friends with the news, but Sam sat quietly with her mother, watching the men unload the truck.

"Maybe we should get three horses," Sam remarked. "Then you can ride with us."

"Oh, no," her mother laughed. "The family next door to me when I was young had horses, so I've ridden quite a bit. But now I am happy to keep my feet on the ground. I'll pet them and give them an apple now and then. But you and Julie will be expected to do most of the work of taking care of them."

"I promise," Sam said happily. "I believed Jim when he said we would get a horse, but I didn't expect it to be so soon."

Mrs. Weirton shook her head. "I think it was that remark you made about a family project."

"Horses would be a great family project," Sam said eagerly. "Except that none of us knows much about them."

"Maybe next week we should see if the library has any books we could use," said Mrs. Weirton. "It will be weeks, maybe months, before we actually get a horse. There will be plenty of time to learn all about them."

CHAPTER EIGHT

"I'VE GOT an idea," said Jim, taking a last slurp of coffee at breakfast. It was a Sunday in mid-October. Sam and Julie were still dressed in their pajamas as they sprawled on the rug in front of the fireplace, reading the Sunday comics. Sam passed the section she had finished to her sister and looked up.

"Why don't we go for a drive and look at horses?" Jim suggested.

Sam caught her breath, but Mom folded the book review section of the paper and shook her head. "Now?"

"Why not?" Jim said.

"Oh, no. You don't know this family. We're suckers for animals. If you took them to the dog pound, they'd want to bring home every dog in the place. And the construction people keep postponing the day they are starting on the barn."

"The construction foreman assured me they would start first thing tomorrow morning," Jim said. "But we are not going to buy a horse today anyway. Buying a horse is a serious matter. We'll have to talk to people, compare breeds. Then we can make a list of things to look for when we are horse-shopping for real. No one would be dumb enough to buy the first horse he sees."

Mom looked reluctant, so Sam spoke up quickly. "It would be fun just to look."

"I know what I want," Julie said. "Something nice and gentle."

"Not me," Sam said firmly. "I want something with a little spirit."

"Here's one," Jim said, circling an ad in the paper. "Small, gentle black horse. Owner going to college."

"What will we do if we find a good horse?" Mom asked. She still sounded hesitant, but Sam could see she was warming to the idea.

"I told you, we will want to look at a lot of horses and compare," Jim said with an airy wave of his hand. "I'll call and make some appointments while you all get ready to go."

Once Jim had an idea, he was a steamroller flattening all opposition. Less than an hour later they pulled up in front of a small neat house at the edge of town.

"This can't be the address," Mom said, checking Jim's notes. "This house has only a tiny yard and no barn."

Just then a girl came walking around the corner of the house, holding a lead rope. A dainty black pony ambled lazily behind. The girl gave the black horse a rather sad look and walked over to greet them.

"Is that the horse for sale?" Jim asked.

The girl nodded. "I'm Karen Reed. My parents have recently moved into town, and as you can see, there isn't enough room here to keep a horse. And I'm going out of state to college, so . . ."

"She's wonderful," Julie said. "What's her name?"

"Beauty. Do you want to ride her? She's really gentle."

Beauty turned calm, patient eyes toward them as they all spilled out of the car and crowded around. "Oh, may I?" Julie asked.

"Have you ridden before?" Karen asked.

"A little bit," Julie answered. "One of my friends in Oregon had a horse."

Mom looked nervous, but Jim nodded. "Not much point in having a pony if you can't ride it."

"I'll walk alongside," Karen told them. Beauty stood quietly as Karen quickly saddled her and slipped on the bridle. Impulsively Julie threw her arms around Beauty's neck. "Oh, she is so perfect."

"She's a little bit fat," Sam said critically.

Julie gave her a dagger-filled look, but Karen chuckled. "That's just the way ponies are shaped. Although Beauty does like to eat. She is a good pony, though," Karen explained. "She has won a lot of ribbons at county fairs. She's very well trained." The pony nuzzled Julie's hand and nickered softly.

"Ohh," Julie squealed in delight. "Her nose feels like velvet."

"She likes you," Karen said, helping her mount.

As Julie slowly rode Beauty around the small yard, Karen walked beside her, giving her tips on riding properly. After a few minutes Julie was ready to try it on her own.

Sam stood watching, trying to push down the waves of jealousy. They looked so right together. Mom and Jim were exchanging glances, and Sam suspected they had already decided to buy Beauty for Julie.

Julie was gaining confidence as she trotted around the small yard. "She's wonderful," she said as she reluctantly dismounted. "This is the one I want."

"Don't forget we agreed to look at all kinds of horses," Jim reminded her. They thanked Karen and climbed back into the car. Julie twisted around in her seat for one last look. "Isn't she the prettiest thing you ever saw?"

Sam turned away from her sister's excited face. "She's all right," she said unenthusiastically. She felt a moment's guilt at the quick hurt look that passed over her sister's face, but secretly she was glad, too. Julie had been acting awful ever since they moved to Ohio, and here Mom and Jim were buying her a pony, just like some sort of reward . . . or bribe.

The next horse was a large, disagreeable Appaloosa, and after that they saw several that proved to be too old, too wild, or otherwise unsuitable. The whole time Julie kept chattering about Beauty.

"She doesn't even have a barn," she said. "All they have is a little shack for her. And she doesn't have enough grass to eat in that little yard."

Mr. and Mrs. Weirton laughed together. "I warned you," Mrs. Weirton said.

Jim looked at Julie in the rearview mirror.

"Maybe next time we look we will find one even nicer."

"I won't find one I like better," Julie insisted. She frowned. "What if we keep looking, and when we go back, someone has already bought her?"

Jim sighed. "Are you absolutely positive?"

"Oh, yes," Julie breathed.

"We'll go back and talk to Karen," Jim said. "Maybe they could hold her until the barn is finished."

"But that's not fair," Sam protested. "I'm the oldest. I should get mine first." *And I deserve it more than Julie,* Sam thought, although she didn't say it out loud.

"But we didn't find one you really liked," Mom said. "We'll go out again."

"It's still not fair," Sam said, scowling.

"You're not being reasonable," Jim said. "We'll find one that's just right for you."

"I hate being reasonable all the time," Sam shouted. She scrunched in the corner of the seat. What if Heather found out that her little sister had a horse and she didn't? It would be just one more humiliation.

Sam leaned her head against the window. What was wrong with her? She knew she was acting like a spoiled little kid. For the first time in a long while they had all been happy together, acting like a family. Now Julie was giving her little hurt looks, and the atmosphere in the car was tense and silent.

"I'm sorry," she said, forcing herself to smile at Julie. "Beauty is a nice horse."

"I would let you ride her until you get yours," Julie said, still looking hurt. She was quiet for a few more minutes, but by the time they reached the Reeds' house, she was chatting as though nothing had happened. The girls stayed outside patting Beauty while their parents talked to Karen's mother and father.

"I wonder how long they will have to keep her before I can bring her home," Julie fretted.

A few minutes later Mom came out of the house, shaking her head and laughing.

"Well, you've got a horse," she told Julie.

Julie jumped and hugged her. "Are we going to pick her up when the barn is built?"

Mom chuckled. "Actually, no. We're getting her tonight."

"Tonight?" Sam could hardly believe her ears. "But . . ."

"They just keep Beauty tied up all the time, so she is used to it. We decided we could do the same thing for the couple of days until we get the barn up. The Reeds have a horse trailer. They will bring her over later."

Jim put his arm around Sam. "I know you're disappointed we didn't find a horse for you today. But Beauty is too good to pass up. We'll find the right one for you."

Sam blushed, remembering her earlier outburst. "It's all right. I guess I was just jealous."

"Karen Reed mentioned a little buckskin quarter horse that might be for sale. We'll go over and look at her soon."

"But we can't bring another horse home until the barn and fence are up," Mrs. Weirton said, looking from her husband to Sam. "Agreed?" she asked sternly.

"Agreed," said Jim.

"Agreed," Sam said reluctantly.

CHAPTER NINE

MONDAY MORNING the phone rang just as Sam sat down for breakfast. Julie answered. "It's the barn contractor," she said, handing the receiver to Jim.

Sam didn't pay any attention to the conversation until she heard Jim mutter, "Oh, no," in an upset tone. She paused with her spoon halfway between her cereal bowl and her mouth.

Jim hung up the phone and ran his fingers through his hair. "They can't come for two more weeks."

"We can just move Beauty around to a new section of grass," Mrs. Weirton said. "The weather's still nice. She'll be all right."

"But I wanted Sam to get her horse soon," Jim said.

Sam shrugged. "It's not your fault. I can wait two more weeks."

Jim beamed at her. "Good girl. Tell you what, tonight as soon as I get home from work we'll go look at that buckskin. I called the owners, and they said they would be willing to hold her for you. That is, if you like her, of course."

Sam nodded, and Jim tweaked her nose affectionately. "Be ready when I get home from work."

"Jim is really a nice guy," Sam said when Mom had left the room with Jim to see him off to work.

"I guess," Julie said listlessly. "If he just wasn't so bossy."

"It's probably hard learning how to be a dad," Sam said.

Julie snorted. "Who made you the great philosopher?"

Sam bit back a sarcastic reply. "I took lessons from Plato," she joked.

Julie smiled. "I guess he is trying to be nice, getting us horses even though he's allergic to them." She was silent for a second. "Do you think our real father would have ever gotten us horses?" she asked hesitantly.

Sam was startled. "I never thought about it. But I don't suppose so. He liked living in the city. He would have thought it over and decided it was too much work or something."

Julie had a strange look on her face. "Can you remember him very much? I mean what he looked like?"

"I have a photo," Sam started to say, but Julie shook her head. "I don't mean that. Sometimes I shut my eyes and try to remember him, and all I can think of is Jim's face. It makes me feel bad. Like I'm being disloyal."

"It's been three years since Dad died in the car accident," Sam said slowly. "I don't think he would mind our having another father. I think he would want us to be happy. I can't remember his face sometimes either. I remember when he taught me how to ride a bike. And that he read me the funny papers on Sunday morning. I remember that he loved us. So wouldn't he want us to be happy? I think he would be glad for us."

Mom came back into the kitchen. "Put a little hay where Beauty can reach it," she said to Julie. "Then after school we'll move her to where she can reach some fresh grass."

Julie finished her glass of milk and went out to the side of the garage where Jim had stacked a few bales of hay the Reeds had given them. Sam followed her and watched. Beauty's ears pricked up and she nickered softly as Julie patted her. "I still can't believe she's mine," she confided. "It's going to be so great when you get your horse, too."

"We're going to be great friends," Julie told Beauty. "I'll see you right after school." She gave her a final pat before they had to run to catch the bus. Jealousy gnawed at Samantha's stomach, but she tried to swallow it down.

"Don't say anything to Mom about what we talked about," Julie said as they climbed on board.

"I won't," Sam promised, waving to Jazz. "I think I have an extra photo I could give you."

"Thanks," Julie said as she made her way to her friends at the back of the bus.

"Was that a horse I saw tied up in your yard?" Jazz asked as Sam slipped into the seat beside her.

"It's Julie's," Sam said. "We just got it yesterday."

"When are you going to get your horse?"

"In two more weeks after they build the barn," Sam said. She twisted around to look at her sister. Julie was talking a mile a minute, telling her friends about her horse. Sam sighed and sank back in the seat.

"It's kind of a bum deal, having your little sister get her horse first," Jazz said sympathetically.

Sam could only nod. She was glad the horse had

made Julie so happy. Sam noticed that Julie had carefully checked that the curling iron was un-plugged, and she had been friendly to Jim at breakfast. But it did seem that Julie always managed to get everything first. First in looks, first to make friends, and even, she thought grimly, the first to get a figure.

At the school's door Jazz waved good-bye. Sam smiled at her. Whatever was wrong in her life wasn't Jazz's fault. She headed for her locker at the other end of the building. Heather was there, taking her books out of her own locker. For once she wasn't surrounded by her friends.

"I forgot all about the library Saturday. I hope you didn't wait too long," she said breezily.

"No. Steven came, and we worked on the report together," Sam said smoothly. Heather frowned and she seemed about to say more, but the first bell rang, and both of them had to dash up the stairs before they were late.

At lunch Jazz talked about the latest pictures she was taking for the photography club, but Sam scarcely listened. She kept noticing that Heather and her friends seemed to be watching her care-fully.

Mrs. Weirton was waiting for Julie and Sam after school. "Let's move Beauty now," she said. "She has eaten all the grass in a big circle around her. Jim's going to get off work early so we can go look at the buckskin."

Sam threw her books on her bed and jumped into an old pair of jeans. Grabbing a jacket, she raced back outside. Jim had found a sturdy ground anchor that screwed into the ground and had a loop on it for tying the rope. Sam untied the rope and held it while her mother pulled the anchor out of the ground and looked around.

"Over by the tree might be a good place," she said, pointing to a spot a few feet away, where the grass was still green in spite of the late season. Beauty followed Sam obediently for a few feet. Then she suddenly stopped and pulled back stubbornly. "Come on," Sam coaxed.

"You have to be firm with her," Mrs. Weirton said encouragingly. "Let her know you're the boss."

Sam tugged harder, but the mare refused to budge. Julie came out of the house, finally finished changing her clothes. "Let me do it," she said. "She'll mind me."

Sam handed her the rope and reached for Beauty's halter. But the little mare whirled suddenly and galloped away before the girls realized what had happened. "Mom," Julie screamed. "She's getting away."

They raced down the road, yelling her name. Tail

flying, Beauty raced away and in a second was out of sight.

"What if she gets lost?" Julie cried as she ran. "What if she gets hit by a car?"

"She won't know where she lives yet," Sam gasped. She was running beside Julie, and she looked almost as stricken.

Then they spied the mare a few feet away in an open field, calmly munching. But as soon as Beauty saw them coming, she took off again.

"This isn't going to work." Mom was panting as she caught up with them. Beauty had stopped again only a few feet further away. "She's playing games with us. Maybe we could circle around her. At least we could turn her toward the house instead of farther away." Mom put her hands on her hips. "I refuse to be outfoxed by a horse."

Beauty made a noise that sounded like a snicker. The pony calmly watched them as she munched a few wild oats that grew along the side of the road.

"Do you need any help?" Sky called from the street in front of his house. He and his sister had seen the mare fly by their house and came running out to join the chase.

"Thanks," Sam called. "We're trying to force her back toward the house."

Jazz and Sky nodded, instinctively understanding what to do. They headed in the opposite direction, making a wide circle and walking slowly, trying to trick the mare into thinking that they weren't after her. But Beauty was too wily for that. Snorting, she kicked up her heels and ran again. This time she did not stop until she had disappeared into a patch of woods.

"I don't know what to do," Mrs. Weirton confessed. "Chasing her seems to be making it worse."

They searched for several more minutes without seeing a sign of the little mare. Finally Mrs. Weirton called a halt. Julie had left the house without a coat and was shivering in the chilly air in spite of all the running.

"Let's go back to the house," said Mrs. Weirton at last.

"We can't just leave her," Julie wailed.

"We won't. Maybe we can get some oats to tempt her with. We'll drive the car to the road on the other side of the woods. Then we can chase her this way."

Weary and discouraged, they trudged up the road. Tears ran down Julie's face, and she wiped at them furiously with her sleeve, ashamed to be crying in front of Sky. Sam put her arm around her sister's shoulder and patted her awkwardly. "Don't worry. We'll catch her," she said comfortingly just as they rounded the corner, bringing the house into view.

Julie was the first to see them. She pointed, wordlessly, to the two figures standing in the driveway. At the same moment Jim saw Julie and the group. Holding Beauty's halter with one hand, Jim waved his other hand in exasperation. "I can't believe all you people would be so careless. The very idea of going for a walk and forgetting to tie up the horse!"

As Beauty's exhausted pursuers sank down on the grass convulsed in laughter, the black mare turned her big brown eyes and calmly looked at them. Later, they all agreed she had looked very pleased with her end of the joke.

CHAPTER TEN

MRS. WEIRTON invited Jazz and Sky to stay for dinner. But after eyeing the hamburger defrosting on the kitchen counter, Jazz insisted they had to go home.

Mom threw together a hasty supper of hamburgers and french fries. Even so, by the time the family had washed and rested from their wild dash and eaten dinner, it was late when they arrived at the farm where the buckskin lived. But the business was concluded in record time. The minute Sam saw the horse, there was no doubt in her mind that this was the one for her.

Cindy was sturdy yet elegant, and her dark golden coat gleamed. She snuffed at Sam's hair over the wooden fence, as though she knew this was her new owner.

"She's really pretty," Julie said. "It's going to be so much fun riding along together."

"Why are you selling her?" Jim asked the owner, Mrs. Hargrove.

"Just plain got too many horses," Mrs. Hargrove said. "I'm running out of pastureland."

"She might be a little young for an inexperienced rider," Jim said hesitantly.

Inwardly Sam moaned, but Mrs. Hargrove shrugged. "She's a gentle little mare. Tell you what. Why don't you leave her here for a while? I'll give her a little extra training. Then if you would like, you can bring your daughter over a few times, and I'll help her work with the horse."

"Oh, Jim, that would be perfect," Sam exclaimed. "And I love her. She'll be just right."

"Are you sure you wouldn't rather start with a slightly older horse?" Mrs. Weirton asked. She scratched Cindy's head and gave her a pat. "She does seem very nice, but you haven't had any experience."

"She's the one I want," Sam pleaded.

"I've got an extra saddle," coaxed Mrs. Hargrove. "How about if I throw that in the deal?"

Jim shook his head and chuckled. "All right. I guess we now own two horses."

Impulsively Sam threw her arms around Jim and hugged him, then her mother. "Oh, thank you, thank you. She's so beautiful."

"Don't worry," Julie said as they climbed back in the car. "You can practice on Beauty until Cindy comes."

"That really worked out well," Jim said. "In a few weeks the barn will be up, and I can have the fencing up, too."

The car lights flashed over Beauty as the car pulled into the drive, and Julie gave a sigh of relief. Sam realized that her sister had been worried the little mare would get loose again. But Beauty appeared quite content and none the worse for her brief taste of freedom. Julie ran to her as soon as the car stopped and handed her a few mouthfuls of hay.

"You know where your home is, don't you, girl?" she said, as Beauty rubbed her head against her.

"I guess she must," Jim said, coming up behind Julie. "She just walked right up to me when I got out of the car. I couldn't believe my eyes."

Julie smiled at him. "Maybe she likes you."

"I like her, too, but—*a-choo*—I don't think I will pet her very much. *A-choo!*"

"You'd better come in, you two," Mom called. "It's getting really nippy out."

"It is starting to get cold for October. I'll bet we

could be in for an early winter," Jim said as they headed for the house. "I hope the contractors get that barn up soon."

Mrs. Weirton made cocoa, and as they sat in the kitchen, still chuckling over the afternoon's chase, Sam felt a warm glow of contentment. Maybe they were on their way to being a family at last.

The good feeling was still with Sam the next day at school. "I'm going to ride Cindy this weekend," she told Jazz at lunch. As usual they were sitting alone. "Mrs. Hargrove said she'd help me learn how to finish training her. Would you like to come with me?"

"I wish I could," Jazz said. "But my photography club is having a real wildlife photographer come and talk to us. He's had pictures in *National Geographic.* I wish you would join," she added.

Sam shrugged. "I guess I'm not into photography," she said. "I like your pictures, though."

"I'd like to take pictures of all the endangered animals in the world. By the time we grow up, it will be too late for some of them," Jazz said seriously.

Sam sighed. It must be nice to know exactly what you were going to do when you grew up. She didn't have the foggiest notion for herself. Sometimes she despaired of ever finding something she was good at doing.

But at least peace reigned at home the rest of the week. When Jim complained about the mess in the bathroom, Julie sweetly promised to clean it up. And when Jim noticed the sack of potato chips Mrs. Weirton had purchased for the girls' lunch bags, he closed the cupboard without comment.

Saturday morning, during breakfast, Jim pulled a piece of paper out of his pocket. "I've been working on this schedule," he began.

Julie and Sam exchanged a look. Even Mrs. Weirton sighed audibly, but Jim ignored her, or else chose not to hear. "I've assigned everyone, including myself, certain jobs. If we all pitch in . . ."

He was interrupted by a loud honk from the drive. "Now who can that be at this time in the morning?" he grumbled.

Sam ran to the window and looked out. "It's a pickup truck," she announced. "And there's a horse trailer attached to it."

With breakfast and schedules forgotten, everyone grabbed a coat and ran outside. "It's Mrs. Hargrove," Julie shouted. "And that's Cindy in the trailer."

Mrs. Hargrove climbed out of the truck. "I'm really sorry to do this," she said, looking embarrassed. "But my husband and I are separating, and I have to move. I won't be able to keep her as I had promised. In fact, if you can't take her now, I'll have to give you your money back and accept another offer."

Jim and Mrs. Weirton exchanged helpless looks. Then they both looked at Sam. As if on cue, she burst into tears. "I knew it," she shouted. "I knew it was too good to be true."

"Now wait a minute," Jim said. "I didn't say we wouldn't take her. We need to think about this for a minute."

Sam kicked at a rock. How many impulsive moves could you expect from a man who did everything according to written schedules?

"Are you sure you couldn't keep her for one more week?" Jim asked. "I hope we'll have the barn started by then. At least it would give me time to put up some fencing."

Mrs. Hargrove shook her head. "I'm flying to my parents' house tomorrow morning."

"It's worked out pretty well with Beauty," Mrs. Weirton said softly. Sam looked up hopefully.

"And it's only for a little more than a week," she added, encouraged by Jim's thoughtful look. "The contractor promised faithfully he'd start on the barn a week from this Monday. And he said it would only take a couple of days to finish."

Jim shook his head. "We must be the only people in the world dumb enough to have two horses without a barn or a fence." He glanced at Sam. "But I guess we don't have much choice."

Mrs. Hargrove led Cindy from the trailer and handed the rope to Sam. Then, apologizing once more, she climbed in her truck and quickly backed out of the drive. Jim went into the garage and returned with a longer rope. "Luckily I bought two of these," he remarked. "It never hurts to be prepared," he added a bit smugly.

"Let's introduce Cindy and Beauty," Julie suggested. Sam led the buckskin over to Beauty. To their surprise, the usually docile black mare wheeled around, snorting in anger. Then she nipped Cindy on the neck. Cindy reared back, startling Sam, who dropped the rope in panic. Cindy galloped a few paces away and stood pawing at the ground.

"Oh, no," Sam wailed. "Not another wild horse chase." But to her surprise, Cindy stood quietly and allowed Mom to take her halter.

"I think we'd better tie them apart for now," she said, patting Cindy until she grew calm. "Let them get used to each other gradually."

But as soon as Jim had Cindy firmly tied in

place, another problem arose. Whereas Beauty seemed to step instinctively over the rope as she moved around, Cindy had obviously never been tied up. As she nervously paced around, she tangled the rope around her legs. Several times Jim walked her around the loops she made in the rope, only to have her tangle herself a second later.

"A-choo," Jim sneezed. "I can't handle these—*a-choo*—horses much—*a-choo*—longer."

"You go in the house, dear," Mrs. Weirton said. "I'll stay out for a while and see if we can't get her calmed down."

"A-choo," Jim sneezed again. "I'm all right if I don't touch them. Maybe if I get away for—*a-choo*—a few minutes, I'll be all right." Jim walked back to the house, sneezing all the way.

Mrs. Weirton looked from her sneezing husband to Cindy, who had tangled herself once more. "Why did we decide we were cowboys?" she asked.

Still agitated by her new surroundings and the rope, Cindy paced, wrapping the rope in a circle around her back leg. Before Mom could walk her out of the loop, she twisted again, pulling the rope tighter. She kicked and fought against the rope, eyes rolling in fear.

"Do something," Sam screamed. "She's hurting

herself." The rope was cutting into Cindy's leg as her panic grew.

"I can't get close enough to grab her," Mom shouted as Cindy stumbled. "Sam, untie the other end of the rope."

Prodded out of her fright, Sam raced to the tree where they had tied the rope and fumbled with the knot. Naturally Jim had tied it impossibly tight. "She's going to break her leg," Julie screamed as Mom grabbed at Cindy's halter, trying to keep her from kicking the rope even tighter. Then with a final tug, Sam worked the knot loose, releasing the buckskin's leg.

Julie was still screaming. "There's blood on her leg." But Mom spoke sharply. "It's just a cut. Go and get Jim."

Jim was already on his way. "I heard the commotion," he yelled. "What happened?"

Mom quickly explained. "I think we should call Mrs. Hargrove back and tell her Cindy is too much for us to handle without a fence. We're not going to be able to tie her to a long rope. I don't know what else to do."

Sam looked desperately at Jim. "Please," she begged, "can't you think of something?"

"Maybe we could tie her to a tree with just enough rope so she can reach her head down to eat hay," Jim said. He frowned at the cut. "We'll have to tend to this," he said. He looked at his wife. "But we have another problem."

Mom looked tired. "I don't think I want to hear this."

"I turned on the radio when I went inside and heard the weather report. It said we are in for a storm, a bad one. They are predicting twelve inches of snow and temperatures below zero before morning.

Mrs. Weirton put her arms around both girls sympathetically as Sam brushed away the hot tears from her eyes. "It isn't fair," she cried.

"Whenever there is a problem, there is a solution," Jim said.

"What is the solution?" Mrs. Weirton asked.

Jim rubbed his hand through his hair. "I said there was a solution. Unfortunately, I don't know what it is," he admitted sheepishly.

CHAPTER ELEVEN

JAZZ SHOOK her head with a disbelieving chuckle. "I always thought my parents were a little peculiar. But yours have them topped any day."

"I'll say," Steven said. He had sat down with them to hear about the new horses. "My mother goes into terminal shock if I even mention getting a dog."

It was three days after the big storm, and they were eating lunch in the cafeteria. The blizzard had been every bit as bad as the weatherman had predicted, and for the last two days the schools had been closed. After two days of confinement, the five hundred middle-school students filled the cafeteria with noisy exuberance.

Sam grinned. She almost had to yell to make herself heard. "Well, they were in a pretty tough spot. Jim is a pain sometimes with all his lists and trying to organize everyone. But when you really have a problem, he's great to have around."

"So tell me," Jazz said. "What did he do?"

"Well, he had Julie and me round up all the wood scraps we could find. And while we were doing that, he shoveled dirt into the garage."

"Wait a minute," Jazz protested. "Why dirt?"

Sky walked by, carrying his tray. He stopped to listen and finally sat down with them. In a cafeteria filled with tables strictly divided between boys and girls, Sam noticed with satisfaction that Heather and her friends had ceased talking and were staring at Sam and Jazz with barely concealed envy.

"Jim said that he had read that horses shouldn't stand on cement for very long." Sam continued her story. "He kept moaning, 'There goes my workshop.' But then he took the scraps we'd found and made two sort of makeshift stalls in the garage. We put some medicine on Cindy's leg and tied the horses up. It worked out great. Our garage is attached to the house," she explained to Steven. "All through the storm we could just walk out the kitchen door and pet the horses. I don't think Mom was real happy about it. She kept running out every few minutes to clean up horse you-know-what. She was afraid it would make the kitchen smell."

Sam chomped the last bit of apple and threw the core in her lunch sack. "Mom says that even though we don't know a lot about horses, we do know three very important things."

"What?" Jazz prodded curiously.

"Horses go a lot. And they go often. And when they do go, it doesn't smell very good."

In the burst of laughter following Sam's observations, she could almost see the three pairs of ears at Heather's table, straining to hear. Heather crumpled up her sack and strolled casually by, pretending she was throwing her trash in the can.

"Did I hear you say you got a horse?" she asked.

Sam nodded. "My sister and I each got one."

"Oh, I'd love to see them," Heather said. "Maybe you could invite me over sometime. I take riding lessons every week. I could probably give you some pointers." Although she was talking to Sam, she looked through her lashes at Sky. "I could teach you, too," she cooed.

"I'm pretty busy with the science club and the rocket club," Sky said.

"Oh, that's even more fascinating," Heather

simpered. "I've always been interested in space. I always watch the television every time they launch the space shuttle."

"I just work with models now," Sky said. "But someday I want to be part of the space program."

"Are you going to be an astronaut?" asked one of Heather's friends, a petite giggly girl named Stacy.

"No," Sky said. "I want to build them, not ride in them." It was plain to see he was flattered by all the attention, but he looked embarrassed, too. He stood up and crumpled his bag. Tossing his sack in the can in a perfect hook shot—showing off a little, Sam thought—Sky made a hasty exit.

Steven followed. "See you around," he said to Sam and Jazz.

"I'll bet you're happy about getting horses," Heather's other friend, a girl named Kirsten, returned to the previous subject. Her smile was open, and a sprinkling of freckles across her nose gave her almost plain features an elfin cuteness. "Did you have horses where you lived before?"

"No," Sam admitted. "We lived by the ocean in Oregon. I had a dog, but my brother kept him. He's going to bring him when he comes for Christmas."

"I'd love to live by the ocean," Kirsten said. "We went there on vacation once. I'll bet you hated to leave."

"We have to go," Heather interrupted before Sam could say more.

Kirsten nodded, but she seemed reluctant to go with her friends. "If you need any help with your horses, tell me. I mean I'm not an expert or anything, but maybe I could help."

"Thanks," Sam called as Kirsten hurried to catch up with Heather.

Sam looked at Jazz, who had not spoken for several minutes. "Kirsten seems kind of nice."

"She is," Jazz said, "if she'd get away from those other two."

"I think Heather likes Sky," Sam giggled. "Did you see the way she was acting around him?"

Jazz snorted. "He's so dumb he can't see what a fake she is. Personally, I don't know why anyone would like him anyway. Most of the time he's a pain in the neck."

"Everybody thinks that about her brother. Mine was, too," Sam said. "But I miss him."

Jazz leaned back in her chair. "If girls were smart, they would talk to a boy's sister before they got married. Bet there would be a lot fewer divorces that way."

Sam laughed. "If they talked to their sisters, there would probably be a lot fewer marriages in the first place."

They gathered up their things just as the bell

rang. Sam hurried to class, wishing for the hundredth time Jazz was in her homeroom. Sam and Steven had become pretty good friends, though none of the girls had been very friendly. But perhaps there was one possibility after all. Kirsten smiled and waved her hand as Sam sat down.

The period after lunch was Sam's favorite part of the day. Mrs. Spritz read to them for fifteen minutes at the beginning of class. Her musical voice made the books come alive, and although some of the kids had complained at first that they were too old to be read to, almost everyone enjoyed it. Today Mrs. Spritz was reading *Roll of Thunder, Hear My Cry*, and even Steven managed to sit quietly. When the teacher put the book down, everyone moaned. Mrs. Spritz rapped her knuckles on her desk. "We'll read more tomorrow. But your geography projects are due a week from tomorrow. I'm going to let you have a few minutes in your groups. You can decide who will do the oral report if you haven't done that already."

After a few minutes of scuffling chairs, the groups settled down to work. Sam held her report. All through the storm she had worked on it, using the notes she had taken at the library. She was pretty sure Mrs. Spritz would be pleased. Sam knew the teacher would also be happy with Steven's wonderful sketches and maps. She was sure the project would earn an *A*. So far Heather had not contributed anything.

"I'd better do the oral report," Heather said.

"That's not fair," Steven protested. "You haven't done a thing to help."

"I knew Sam was writing the report and you were doing the pictures. What else was there to do? Besides, I'm pretty good at oral reports," Heather said.

Steven opened his mouth to say more, but Sam quickly handed Heather the report. "It's all right," she told Steven. "I don't really want to stand up in front of everyone."

Heather skimmed through the report. "Hey, this looks really good."

"No thanks to you," Steven mumbled.

Heather ignored him and dropped the report on her desk. "Are you going to the dance?" she asked Sam.

"What dance?"

"Washington Middle School has three dances during the year. The first one is just before Thanksgiving."

Sam shook her head. "I probably won't go."

"Do you think Sky will go?"

"I don't know," Sam answered honestly.

"Does he ever say anything about me?"

"No," Sam said shortly.

"Would you ask him if he likes me?" Heather asked.

Sam stared at her in amazement. Did Heather really think she would help her after the way she'd been acting? But Heather sat looking perfectly innocent, waiting for an answer.

"No," Sam said firmly.

They had forgotten about Steven. Now he suddenly crowed with laughter. Even in a room filled with the murmur of group discussions, his laughter rang out loud and clear.

Mrs. Spritz tapped her pencil on the desk. "I didn't know geography was such an amusing subject."

"Sorry, Mrs. Spritz," Steven answered, still grinning broadly. "We just thought of something neat to do for our project."

"I will be looking forward to it with great anticipation," Mrs. Spritz said dryly. There was a twinkle in her eyes when she spoke. Sam suspected that even though she often scolded Steven, he was one of her favorites.

"Now you've done it," Heather almost growled. "She'll be thinking we're going to do something really great."

Steven shrugged. "Then let's see." He paused, thinking. "We could pretend everyone in the room is on a tour bus."

"That's a great idea," Sam told him. "I could bring some tortilla chips and guacamole to pass out."

Steven leaned over to Sam. "If you do go to the dance, I'll dance with you."

"I'm sure that gives her a thrill," Heather sneered.

Sam saw the quick hurt look pass over Steven's face. "I think that would be nice," she said quickly.

Mrs. Spritz signaled for the students to return to their seats. "Do you think Jazz will go with you?" Steven asked as they carried their chairs back to their places.

"Do you like Jazz?" Sam asked, surprised but pleased.

Steven shrugged nonchalantly. "She's pretty interesting, for a girl. You are, too," he added quickly. "But you and I are more like friends."

"I'll see what I can do," Sam promised.

CHAPTER TWELVE

"**I** JUST CAN'T," Jazz said, shaking her head violently, as they were riding the bus to school. Sam had been trying to convince Jazz for a whole week to go to the dance.

"Steven really wants you to come," Sam insisted. "And so do I."

For the first time since Sam had met her, Jazz seemed unsure of herself. The ongoing discussion about the dance had thrown her into a panic.

"Look," Jazz said. "I know I'm not like most other people. Everyone thinks I'm kind of weird. That's okay. I just go about my business and do my own thing. But this would be like going into their territory. You understand what I'm saying?"

Sam nodded. "But it's not like you'll be alone.

I'm nervous about going, too. I don't think I'd be brave enough by myself. And Steven's kind of weird, too. But nice," she added, seeing Jazz's look.

"I don't have anything to wear."

"I've got a green sweater that would look great on you," Sam offered.

"I'll think about it," Jazz promised. "Do you know how to dance?"

Sam shook her head. "Not really."

"Sky goes to the dances. Maybe he could teach us."

"I'd be too embarrassed," Sam said.

"You like him," Jazz hooted, while Sam blushed furiously. Then she stopped laughing. "I'm sorry. I'm not laughing at you. It's just that I always think of him as such a pain. I know what we could do. I'll have him teach me, then I'll come over and teach you."

"Do you think he likes me?" Sam asked shyly.

Jazz nodded. "He said you were a lot of fun the night we played Scrabble. Probably because you laughed at his dumb jokes."

The bus wheezed to a stop, and Sam's good mood vanished. This was the geography presentation day. What if Heather ruined all their hard work by not being prepared? But she needn't have worried. Heather was magnificent. Even Steven rolled his eyes in surprise. Heather had dressed a little like a tour guide in a straight skirt and jacket and a fancy sombrero she said her parents had brought back from a trip to Mexico. For the display, she had brought some turquoise-and-silver bracelets and a charm bracelet with Aztecan designs. While Steven and Sam passed out the chips and dip they had brought, Heather pointed out the places of interest. Holding up Steven's paintings, Heather even described the customs of the Aztecs and of the Mayan and Toltecan people. When she finished, everyone clapped, and Mary Frances turned around to Sam. "You guys did a really good job," she said.

"That was wonderful." Mrs. Spritz clapped her hands.

"Thank you," Heather said, sounding modest. "I learned a lot about Mexico when my parents took a trip there. That's where I got the silver jewelry and the sombrero."

Sam couldn't believe her ears. Heather was making it sound as though she had done all the work. She caught Steven's eye. He looked disgusted, but he shrugged as though he had expected it.

Mrs. Spritz beamed at the class. "We're off to a wonderful start. I just hope the rest of the reports will be as entertaining and informative."

When the bell rang for lunch, Mrs. Spritz motioned for Sam to stay. "I really liked the way your report was written. The seventh and eighth grades write the school newspaper, but they need someone in the sixth grade to write the sixth-grade news. Would you be interested?"

Sam was so surprised her mouth fell open. "How did you know I wrote the report?"

"Heather is good at theatrics, but she needs a little work on her writing skills. And Steven of course is a wonderful artist. I wouldn't be surprised if he became famous someday. But he, too, needs to work on writing. So that leaves you." Mrs. Spritz winked. "A teacher must also be a detective sometimes."

Sam nodded. "I'd love to write for the paper."

"Good," Mrs. Spritz said briskly. "Now for an idea. Why don't you ask people what they think of middle school. You know, things like, is it what they expected, what kinds of problems have they encountered. That sort of thing. It might help you get to know some people," she added when Sam looked hesitant.

"I guess I could try it," Sam agreed.

"That's wonderful," said Mrs. Spritz. "I'll tell them we've found our reporter."

"I thought today was going to be awful, but this morning ended up being totally terrific," Sam told

Jazz at lunch. "There's just one more thing to do to make the day perfect."

"What's that?" Jazz asked.

"If Jim is done building the fence, I'm finally going to ride Cindy tonight," Sam answered.

"It's about time," Jazz said. "You've had her almost two weeks."

"The weather's been bad," Sam said. "And Jim was worried that Cindy might be nervous with all the lumber for the barn piled around."

"That's great. But are you scared about riding?"

"Why would I be scared to ride my own horse?" Sam said boldly. Then she blushed. "Well, maybe a little."

"*I* would be," Jazz said. "I sat on a horse once. You feel like you are terribly far from the ground."

"Thanks a lot," Sam said.

Jazz poked her playfully with an elbow. "Mind if I come over and watch? I need a good laugh."

Sam agreed, but later, while Mrs. Weirton helped her saddle Cindy, she looked up to see both Jazz and Sky walking across the field, and her heart sank.

"Oh, no," she said under her breath. "Sky's coming, too. What if I do something dumb?"

"I'm sure he is just trying to be friendly," her mother said. "You'll be fine. Just remember how I showed you to handle the reins."

"I'll remember," Sam said as she put her foot in the stirrup. Putting her weight on the stirrup, she tried to swing her other leg over. She found that she couldn't. Grunting with the effort, she tried again. This time the whole saddle slid down. Sam ended up in a heap on the ground, and the saddle, still fastened by the girth strap, ended up hanging under Cindy's belly.

Sky gave a loud guffaw. "You planning to ride that horse upside down, cowboy?" he asked in a loud drawl.

"Be quiet, Sky," Jazz said, but she was unable to keep her own laughter out of her voice.

Sam bristled. Then, seeing the saddle hanging, she felt a smile twitch at the corners of her mouth.

"I guess we need a little practice saddling horses," Mrs. Weirton chuckled.

"Let me help," Sky offered gallantly. "I've ridden a few times at a friend's house. He showed me this little trick."

Cindy stood patiently while he righted the saddle. He unbuckled the girth strap and slapped Cindy on the stomach. A whoosh of air came out of her nostrils, and Sky jerked the strap tight.

"They puff out their stomach sometimes," Sky explained as he worked. "It's a little trick horses play."

Sam put her foot back up in the stirrup and

tried to mount. But again she couldn't get her leg over. Trying not to look completely ridiculous, she held onto the saddle horn and gave a mighty leap up. This time she managed to get her leg over. And then, before she could gain her balance, her other leg followed. Unable to stop the motion, she slid completely over the top of Cindy's back and plopped on the ground with a hard thump!

"Are you all right?" Mrs. Weirton came rushing around with a worried look. Jazz and Sky were right behind her. Sam looked at the three concerned faces peering down at her. Realizing how ludicrous she must look, Sam rolled back on the cold ground and gave herself up to giggles. Relieved to see her unhurt, the others joined in. "Maybe we can give you a push up," Mrs. Weirton said when the laughter was under control.

Sam picked herself up. "I can't have someone help me every time I want to ride my horse," she said with new determination.

"Maybe if you climb up on the gate, you can swing over from there," Jazz offered.

"That's a great idea." Sam nodded. "Why didn't I think of that before I gave myself all these bruises?" She tied Cindy to the new rail gate at the barn's entrance. She climbed up and swung her leg over, but just as she did, Cindy moved her hind end away from the gate. Sam was left doing a split in midair, one foot still on the gate, the other on Cindy's back.

Seeing her dilemma, Sky rushed over and pushed Cindy's rump until Sam could slide herself over.

"So much for that idea," she said, feeling her face burn as she settled into place.

Now that she was actually astride her horse, she understood what Jazz had meant. The ground did seem awfully far away. When Cindy took a step forward, Sam grabbed the saddle in panic.

"Looking good," Sky called encouragingly.

"Just walk her until you have more experience," Mrs. Weirton called. "Give her a little kick."

"What if she bucks?" Sam asked, nearly frightened to tears.

"She won't," soothed Mrs. Weirton. "Just let her walk."

Sam was too embarrassed to look at Jazz and Sky. But the thought of them watching finally gave her the courage to try. Still hanging on for dear life, she lightly prodded Cindy into a walk.

"Relax a little," called Mrs. Weirton as Sam clung to the saddle horn, white faced and shaking. Sam grimly hung on. Gone were the dreams of wild midnight gallops. Now all she could think about was surviving this terrible afternoon.

Another fifteen minutes and her mother called

a halt just as Julie came out of the house. Sam swung her leg over and jumped down. Getting off a horse was much easier than getting on. She patted Cindy to hide her shaking hands.

"I was just coming out to ride with you," Julie said. Sam was glad her sister had not seen the lesson's disastrous beginning. Julie had already ridden Beauty several times. In fact, Jim had remarked that Julie had taken to riding as though she had been born in the saddle.

There was a strange weakness on the inside of Sam's legs, and she could hardly walk. "I think I've had enough for today," she said.

"You did really great for your first time," Jazz said.

"You said you needed a laugh," Sam said a bit ruefully.

"You're a good sport," Sky said. "Some girls would have just given up."

"Why would they give up?" Julie asked.

"Your sister had a tiny problem getting on her horse," Mrs. Weirton explained. Sam glared at her, but Mrs. Weirton didn't seem to notice that she was upset. At least she didn't mention how afraid Sam had been.

"I just put my foot in the stirrup and swing the other leg over," Julie said smugly. "Beauty always stands perfectly still for me."

"Cindy is a bigger horse," Mrs. Weirton explained. "And it was partly my fault. We didn't get the saddle on tight enough."

Glumly Sam listened as her mother explained the whole disaster. Now she would have to listen to Julie brag about how much better she could ride. Sam knew that what was really upsetting her was the fear. When she had pictured herself riding, she had never imagined she would be afraid. Now that she was on firm ground again, she wasn't sure that she could force herself to even try riding again.

"I have trouble getting the saddle on Beauty, too," Julie admitted. "She's getting awfully fat."

Sky showed her the trick to saddle the horse just as Jim arrived home. The story had to be repeated for him, of course, but Sam didn't stay to listen. She led Cindy into her stall in the new barn and gave her a handful of grain for a treat.

"Sounds like you had quite a ride," Jim said as he walked through the open barn door.

"I didn't mean for it to be the afternoon's entertainment," Sam snapped.

"Reminds me of when I was trying to learn to ride a bike. I lived in kind of a rough neighborhood, and most of the kids were older than me. I wasn't the most graceful kid in the world. By the time I finally mastered the bike, I was skinned in places I didn't even know you could skin yourself. And every time I practiced, every kid in the neighborhood gathered around for a laugh."

"Is this one of those stories that is supposed to teach me something?" Sam asked.

Jim grinned. "Not really. Just wanted to let you know that I understand how you feel."

"I guess I did look pretty silly." Sam managed to smile.

"There is one thing," Jim said. He hesitated before he continued. "When all those boys were standing around watching, I was so tense and nervous that I knew I would never learn. So I started getting up very early and practicing by myself. Then one day I just got on my bike and rode down the street in front of everyone."

"I didn't know riding a horse could be so scary," Sam said softly.

"Bike, horse, car, whatever. It's all scary until you learn. You just have to decide who's the boss. But to this very day I can remember that feeling as I rode my bike in front of those boys. It was worth any amount of scary."

Sam looked at him. "I'll do it," she declared with new determination.

"I never doubted it for a minute," Jim said.

Sam gave him a rueful smile. "I did."

CHAPTER THIRTEEN

"**I** DIDN'T MEAN to laugh." Jazz apologized for the third time when she visited on Friday evening.

Sam slipped the movie into the VCR. "It's all right. I know it must have looked hysterical," she said. "But I'm going to get up early tomorrow morning and practice. Next time you see me, I'll be riding like an expert."

Sam hit the fast-forward button to roll the movie past the credits. Jazz leaned forward, watching. "It looks kind of fun actually. I didn't think I would ever like to ride, but after watching you, I think I might."

"You could come over and help me learn to ride

Cindy," Sam offered. "I'm going to practice in the mornings until I learn. If you come, at least somebody will be there to call an ambulance when I fall off and break my neck," she said grimly.

"Wait," Jazz almost shrieked. "There's a kiss. Stop the film."

Sam rewound the movie and hit "pause" just as the man and the woman were about to kiss. "Nope, no good," Jazz said. "Her back is to us. You can't see how she has her lips."

"She has her head bent just a little, though," Sam said. "That must be how they get around each other's nose."

Sam started the movie on fast-forward again. "There must be lots more kisses. Mom said all these movies were very romantic."

"You told your mother you wanted to watch movies to learn how to kiss?" Jazz asked incredulously.

Sam grinned. "Actually, I told her I was trying to write a romantic story for English."

Jazz sounded relieved. "Did she believe you?"

"She looked at me kind of funny," Sam admitted. "Wait. Here's another kiss."

They watched in silence as the movie lovers kissed a long, passionate kiss. "I don't think I could kiss like that," Jazz gulped.

"It looked like he was biting her instead of kissing," Sam said.

"Maybe the first time all you have to do is peck. You know, like you kiss your mom and dad," Jazz offered. She hit her hand on her head. "Boy, are we dumb. You can watch your mom and Jim. If they haven't been married very long, they probably still kiss romantically."

"I don't like to watch them," Sam answered shortly.

"These movies are not helping very much," Jazz said, switching the player off. "Maybe we should just forget the whole thing. If we don't get boyfriends, then we don't ever have to worry about it."

"I wonder if boys ever worry about things like that," Sam said.

"Sky always leaves the room in the mushy parts of movies. He says it makes him want to throw up."

"If you want to learn how to kiss, you should practice," Julie said, slyly slipping into the room.

"How long have you been snooping?" Sam yelled.

"Long enough," Julie answered. "If you want to learn how to kiss, just practice on a mirror. That's what I do."

"You actually kiss a mirror?" Jazz asked.

125

"That's the stupidest thing I ever heard," Sam said disgustedly.

"I'm never giving you any more help," Julie said, flouncing out of the room.

"Would you like to stay for dinner?" Mrs. Weirton asked, sticking her head around the door. Seeing Jazz's hesitation, she smiled. "Macaroni. And a salad."

"Thanks." Jazz nodded, accepting the invitation.

"Did you learn anything from the movies?"

"Not really. They were a little *too* romantic, I think," Sam said.

The girls followed Sam's mother back to the kitchen. Sam handed the dishes to Jazz to set the table. "Do you remember your first kiss?" Sam asked.

Mrs. Weirton nodded. "Harold Kravitz."

"Harold Kravitz?"

Mrs. Weirton nodded. "He had walked me down to the ice cream shop one Saturday afternoon. When we got back, we sat on the porch swing and he kissed me."

Sam tried to picture her mother sitting on a porch swing with a boy. "What did you do?" she asked.

"Nothing. I was too surprised. Then my dad swung open the door. I guess he scared poor Harold to death. Harold jumped up and almost ran down the road."

"How did you know how to kiss?" Jazz asked.

Mrs. Weirton chuckled. "I guess it just comes naturally."

Sam frowned. That was all right for some people. But what if it didn't come naturally to everyone? Her eyes met Jazz's, and she knew Jazz was wondering the same thing.

"Are you girls thinking about kissing someone?" Mrs. Weirton asked.

"No," Sam answered quickly. "I'm just gathering material for my story."

"That must be some story," Mrs. Weirton said mildly.

All through dinner, Sam watched Julie, afraid she would tell what she had overheard. But Julie was too busy chatting about her school project.

"We're having a school carnival, and I've been picked to be the games chairman," she announced.

"That sounds like fun," Mom said, "but a lot of responsibility."

Julie nodded glumly. "A room mother will help me, but I don't know where to start."

"Why not make a list of all the possibilities?" Jim said. "Like ringtoss, fishing, and so on. Then you'll need another list of necessary equipment. I would imagine the school has most of what you need left over from other carnivals."

"Would you help me make the lists?" Julie asked shyly.

Jim nodded. "You could ask some of the other children what games they liked best at other carnivals, but we could start right after dinner."

"Bingo," Jazz offered.

"Maybe some of the parents could bake cupcakes, and you could have a cakewalk," Jim suggested.

Sam was almost ready to help when she saw a smile pass between Julie and Jim. Maybe this was just what they needed. She could tell from her mother's face that she felt the same way. Mrs. Weirton hummed as she picked up the dirty dishes from the table.

CHAPTER FOURTEEN

BEFORE SHE left that evening, Jazz had promised to help Sam practice her riding. True to her word, Jazz was sitting on the back steps when Sam slipped outside the following morning. "Why didn't you knock?" Sam said. "I didn't know you were here."

"I didn't want to wake your family in case you changed your mind."

"Chickened out, you mean."

"Yeah." Jazz grinned at her. "But I knew you wouldn't."

"Don't think that I didn't think about it," Sam said. "But all my life I've dreamed of having my own horse. It seems kind of dumb to throw it all away when my dream has come true. I guess sometimes we don't realize how scary some of those dreams can be."

Cindy was waiting by the gate. She nickered softly when she saw Sam. Sam snapped the rope on her halter and led her out. She shook her finger at Cindy and scolded. "Now, listen. I'm going to ride you, and furthermore, I am going to enjoy it."

Cindy's soft eyes watched as Sam and Jazz together put the saddle on and tightened the girth. Remembering Sky's trick from the day before, Sam slapped Cindy's belly. Her breath was released with a whoosh, and Jazz jerked the girth strap tight.

"Why don't you put your foot in the stirrup and then stand up before you even try swinging your leg over?"

Sam followed Jazz's suggestion and managed to mount, if not gracefully, at least without falling over. The whole practice went better. Sam was even able to relax a little, and she rode several times around the pasture with Jazz cheering her on.

"Definitely an improvement over the other day," Jazz said approvingly.

"Do you want to take a turn?" Sam asked as she slid off.

Jazz glanced at her watch. "Better not. Mom's

taking me to town to buy some equipment for my darkroom."

"Did you decide about the dance?"

Jazz nodded. "I'll go. But just because we're friends. I know I'm not going to like it." She waved good-bye as she headed home.

"Where are you going?" Julie asked. She had been on her way to the barn and had overheard.

"The middle-school dance," Sam answered.

"You are so lucky." Julie sighed. She leaned on the gate and watched Beauty. "They had dancing at Lauren's party. The one Mom and Jim made me miss."

"That was too bad you had to miss it," Sam said.

Julie shrugged. "Her parents weren't home. The party got so loud that the neighbors called the police, and all the parents had to go to the police station and pick up the kids."

Sam just stared at Julie. "Then Jim really kind of saved you," she said at last.

Julie nodded. "Do you think I should tell him?"

"I think that would make him happy," Sam answered.

"Maybe I will," Julie said. "I'll think about it." She looked back at her pony. "Don't you think Beauty is getting kind of fat?"

"Maybe you are feeding her too much," Sam suggested. "Or maybe she needs more exercise."

"I ride her almost every day," Julie protested. "And I'm feeding her just what the books say."

"What are you two doing?" Jim called in a friendly voice as he headed down the driveway to get the mail.

"I was talking about how fat Beauty is," Julie called back.

"She's right," Sam said as Jim cut across the lawn and joined them. "I've noticed it, too."

Jim ran his fingers through his hair. "Come to think of it, I have noticed she's a little plump. Maybe we had better have the vet out to take a look."

"Do you think something could be wrong with her?" Julie asked anxiously.

"No," Jim said reassuringly. "We're probably feeding her too much. Unless . . ." He gave Beauty a critical look but didn't finish his sentence.

"Unless what?" Julie asked, her face scrunched with worry.

Jim shook his head. "Nothing to worry about. I was just thinking that she looks a little like she might be going to have a baby. But let's wait till the vet comes."

A small muddy pickup truck was in the driveway when Sam and Julie got home from school on Monday.

"That must be the vet," Julie said as she broke into a run for the barn.

"Girls, this is Dr. Johnson," said their mother as they burst through the barn door.

Dr. Johnson snapped his bag closed. "Those are two fine horses, Mrs. Weirton. Fit as a fiddle. I can see you are taking good care of them."

"You don't think Beauty is a little too fat?" questioned Mrs. Weirton.

"Well, not for her condition," Dr. Johnson said, patting the small black mare. Tiny crinkles appeared around his bright blue eyes when he smiled.

Mrs. Weirton hesitated. "What do you mean?"

"I'd say Beauty's going to have a little one. And soon. Maybe by Christmas."

"A baby?" Mrs. Weirton croaked while her daughters did a little dance of joy.

"I can't be one hundred percent sure," Dr. Johnson continued. "I didn't actually hear a heartbeat. But judging by all the signs, it won't be too long."

"A baby," Sam and Julie squealed together when Dr. Johnson had climbed in his truck and roared down the drive. "Won't that be great?"

"Great," said Mrs. Weirton. Then she brightened. "I guess it will be kind of a nice nature lesson. We can always sell it when it gets older."

"Sell it?" Sam wailed. "It's not even born and you are already giving it away."

"We certainly don't need *three* horses," Mrs. Weirton said firmly.

"Maybe you could ride it," Julie suggested.

"Forget it. I like to keep both my feet on the ground," said their mother.

"I have a great idea," Sam said thoughtfully. "We could take pictures and then I could write a book. There are contests for kids. If you win, they publish your book. Mrs. Spritz thinks I might have a talent for writing."

"That sounds neat," Julie said. Generously she added, "You could borrow my camera."

"I'll bet Jazz would help me," Sam said, warming to the idea. "She takes great pictures."

"I'm not sure that we know enough about horses to write a book," warned Mrs. Weirton. "But it might be fun to try. In the meantime, Sam, will you let Julie ride Cindy? Dr. Johnson said it was all right to keep riding Beauty, but I think we should let her have a rest. We want to have a good healthy baby for that story."

"Sure," Sam agreed quickly.

Mrs. Weirton went back in the house, humming something Sam thought might have been "Home on the Range."

"Looks like our family project is turning this

place into MacDonald's farm," Jim joked when they told him the news.

"I didn't know this would happen when I suggested a project," Sam remarked.

Jim winked. "It's working, isn't it?"

Sam glanced at Julie, who was happily making plans with her mother for the big event while she set the table for dinner, and smiled at Jim. The past few weeks had been peaceful except for an occasional normal family squabble. *Family.* It had a nice sound to it. "I think so," she answered.

"I have some more good news," Mrs. Weirton said, as she stirred a pot of chili on the stove. "Your brother is going to fly home for Thanksgiving."

"So much is happening," Sam exclaimed. "The new baby horse, Kevin coming, my first dance."

"Dance!" Jim exclaimed. And grabbing his wife, he whirled her around the room.

"I'm dripping the chili all over the floor," Mrs. Weirton protested, still holding onto her serving spoon. But she followed his lead gracefully, dipping and swaying to imaginary music.

Sam was delighted. "I didn't know you could dance like that," she said as her mother whirled by.

"Ha!" Jim said. "I'll have you know that three girls signed my high school yearbook 'To the

dreamiest dancer at John Davis High School.' "
He leered at Mrs. Weirton. "Jealous?" he asked
wickedly.

"On rainy days when there was square dancing
during recess at P.S. Forty-two, who do you think
the most popular girl was?" Mrs. Weirton shot
back. "The boys stood in line to dance with me."

"Did you have to do that, too?" Julie asked in a
delighted voice. "That's what we have to do."

"Well, then," Jim said, shooing his wife back to
the stove, "get back to your stirring. I have a new
partner." He grabbed Julie and did a perfect do-si-
do around the kitchen.

Sam clapped her hands, aware that she was
grinning from ear to ear. "Do you think that you
could teach me to dance?" she asked her parents.
"Jazz is going to help me a little, but maybe you
could, too."

"Certainly," Jim said. "The line forms to the
right." He switched on the radio as he danced by
with Julie. By the time Mrs. Weirton called them to
sit down for dinner, both of the girls could manage
to follow his lead without tripping over their feet.

Sam told Jazz about the impromptu dance the
next morning on the bus. "I'll teach you what Jim
and Mom teach me, and you can show me what
you learn from Sky. By the time we go to the dance,
we'll probably be the best dancers there."

Jazz looked a little grim. She voiced the nagging worry in Sam's mind when she said, "Let's just hope we have a chance to show off what great dancers we are."

CHAPTER FIFTEEN

THE NIGHT of the dance Sam stared at her reflection in the mirror and frowned. "I wish I wasn't so skinny," she said.

"You look nice," Julie said as she combed a last curl into place.

"Well, my hair looks nice. Thanks to you," Sam said. "But my legs look like toothpicks, and I must be the only girl in sixth grade who doesn't have a figure."

"You have a figure," Julie said.

"Yeah," Sam giggled. "But it's more like a Popsicle stick than a girl."

"I wouldn't care what kind of figure I had if I could go to the dance," Julie said wistfully.

For the first time Sam felt older than her sister. The idea of going to a dance with seventh and eighth graders made her nervous, but at the same time she felt very grown-up. She only hoped she didn't end up standing alone all night. Just thinking about the possibility made her stomach turn. When she closed her eyes, she could almost see herself standing on the sidelines while Heather and her friends danced by with pitying looks. But surely that couldn't happen. Steven had promised to dance one dance with her. And maybe Sky would, too.

"You had better hurry up," Jim called from the stairs. "We will be late picking up Jazz and Sky." Jim had volunteered to drive them to the dance and pick them up when it was over.

"Why, Miss Samantha, you look positively gorgeous," Jim drawled when she hurried downstairs.

Sam flashed him a nervous grin and waved good-bye to her mother and Julie. "Have fun," Mrs. Weirton said with a smile.

Outside, the air was frigid, and little frost puffs formed around her nose when she breathed. She pulled her coat around her and hurried to the car. "You won't make a big fuss or anything in front of Jazz or Sky, will you?"

Jim winked at her. "After the dance I will come

into the school and yell, 'I'm looking for my little girl so I can give her a ride!' " he said. "That way you can find me for sure in the crowd."

Sam gasped in horror. "You wouldn't really do that."

Jim laughed as he pulled the car into the McKennas' drive. "I'm not that old. I'll be so discreet you'll think the car is driving itself."

Samantha impulsively leaned over and kissed his cheek. "You are turning into a pretty good dad," she said softly.

Jim gave her a pleased look. "That's the first time you've called me Dad. I like it."

Jazz and Sky were ready and waiting when the car pulled up in front of their house. "This is going to be a total disaster," Jazz moaned. "Why did I let you talk me into going?"

"You look great," Sam told her.

"So do you," Sky whispered.

"We'll be the greatest-looking bunch of wall huggers you ever saw," Jazz said with a sigh.

Sky shrugged. "If it's really awful, we'll just call Sam's dad and go home and play Monopoly."

The eighth-grade decorating committee had managed to make the usually drab gym look almost cheerful with the winter theme, and the music was so loud Sam could feel the sound waves. She grinned at Jazz. "I think this is going to be fun."

"Maybe," Jazz said, not quite convinced. She looked around the room. Most of the kids were still standing around, looking nervous, but a few brave couples were already on the floor.

"Everyone just throws their coats in the corner," Sky shouted over the music. He led them to the back wall, and Jazz and Sam added their coats to the giant heap on the floor.

"Do you know how to dance?" he asked Sam.

"A little bit," she said. "Jim's been teaching me."

"We'll be back in a minute," Sky told his sister. He took Sam's hand and led her to the middle of the room, where the other couples were dancing. Samantha was so nervous she wondered if Sky could feel her shaking. At least it was a slow song. Maybe she could follow without falling over his feet.

But it was Sky who tripped over hers. The second time he did it, he was so apologetic that Sam had to laugh. "I was worried I'd be tripping over your feet," she admitted.

"I guess I'm kind of nervous," Sky said.

"Why are you nervous?" Sam asked, truly surprised.

"Dancing with pretty girls always makes me

141

nervous," Sky said just as the music ended.

He held her hand as they squeezed through the crowd to find Jazz. Sam was worried she might be feeling left out but quickly saw that Steven had found her. The four of them pushed their way to one of the few tables set up in a corner.

Heather was there, surrounded by all her friends. "Hello, Sky," she cooed. "Are you going to dance with me?"

"I already promised to dance with Sam again," Sky said. He jumped up and almost pulled Sam back to the dance floor.

"You can dance with her if you want," Sam said, trying to sound like she meant it.

"I don't want to," Sky said firmly. "I'd much rather dance with you."

They worked their way over to Jazz and Steven, energetically doing a fast dance. It was obvious Steven had never danced before, but Jazz was laughing so hard she could hardly keep up.

"I'm glad you talked Jazz into going tonight," Sky said. "She's a little shy about things like this. I'm glad you're her friend." He cleared his throat nervously. "I've been wanting to ask you some-thing. Would you like to be my girlfriend?"

Sam could hardly believe her ears. "Yes." She nodded happily.

When the song was over Sam grabbed Jazz

by the arm. "We have to go comb our hair," she said.

"We do?" Jazz asked. But seeing Sam's barely concealed excitement, she nodded.

The rest rooms were crowded with girls, but Sam pulled Jazz into a corner by the mirror. "Sky asked me to go with him."

Jazz nodded. "He told me he was going to ask you. Guess what? Steven asked me to go with him."

Sam was so happy she couldn't resist whirling Jazz around in a dance of joy.

Several of the girls from her homeroom were at the sink, combing their hair, and overheard. "That's great," Mary Frances exclaimed, looking as if she really meant it.

Kirsten turned from the mirror, comb in midair. "Heather's not going to be happy to hear that," she said. "She likes him, too. She's been telling everyone that he's her boyfriend." She didn't look as though she felt very sorry for Heather.

"What are you talking about?" Heather asked as she walked through the door.

Kirsten looked uncomfortable. "Sky just asked Sam to go with him."

Heather's eyes shot daggers. "Probably it's just because you're friends with his weirdo sister," she said, even though Jazz was listening.

"Your idea of not being weird seems to be being snotty to someone new in school and taking the credit for work someone else has done." Sam was so angry her voice cracked. "To you, being weird means being interested in things and being a kind and good friend. I'll take weird any day."

Heather's lips curled down in a sneer. "Of course you would. You're just as weird as Jazz. You two deserve each other."

"That's the nicest thing anyone ever said to me," Sam said. She grabbed Jazz's hand and pulled her through the door. "Come on, there's an awful smell in here."

Sam stood outside the door, still shaking with anger. "It's okay," Jazz said. "Thanks for sticking up for me. But people like her are not worth bothering about."

"I wanted tonight to be perfect," Sam said. She was calmer now but sad. Only a few minutes before the gym had seemed like a winter dream. Now suddenly it seemed shabby and dull.

"Sam, Jazz, wait!" called a voice. It was Kirsten. "That was a terrible thing Heather said in there. I just told her so, too." She smiled shyly. "I didn't want you to think everyone was like that." She paused. "Heather was real popular in fifth grade. I thought I was really lucky when she picked me to be part of her club. But maybe middle school is a good time to make new friends."

Sam snapped her fingers. "I'm supposed to write an article for the newspaper. Would you let me interview you?"

Kirsten nodded. "That would be neat. I know some other girls who would probably do it, too."

Sky and Steven made their way through the crowd. "Come on," Sky said, taking Sam's hand. "We've missed four dances."

"See you at school," Kirsten called after them.

Sam felt as if she was in a dream. Sky danced almost every dance with her, and when it was over, he held her hand as they walked out to the car. If Jim noticed, he kept his promise and stayed discreetly silent. And unlike Harold Kravitz, who ran when he saw Sam's mother's father, Sky kept on holding Sam's hand until Jim dropped him and Jazz off at their house.

CHAPTER SIXTEEN

ON THANKSGIVING morning Sam stretched luxuriously under the covers. Four whole days that she didn't have to get up early! She tried to get back to sleep, but the spicy smells of pumpkin pie and turkey stuffing made her stomach growl. She sat up in bed when it hit her. Thanksgiving! That meant her brother, Kevin, would be here anytime.

She leaped into her clothes and ran downstairs. Julie was already stirring Jell-O for fruit salad.

"Jim's gone to the airport to pick up Kevin," Mrs. Weirton said. "After breakfast you can give the horses their grain, so it will be done when they get back."

Sam gulped down a bowl of cereal and struggled into her coat and boots. She hurried to the barn, her feet crunching on the light dusting of newly fallen snow.

Usually Cindy and Beauty were waiting eagerly for their morning grain, but Sam had to call several times before Cindy came in alone. She seemed agitated and only grabbed one mouthful before she hurried back out the door that led to the pasture.

"What's the matter, girl?" Sam asked. "And where is that Beauty this morning?" She walked around the barn to see why Beauty hadn't come to eat.

There was a flash of something white and a flick of tail. "Well, no wonder you're nervous," Sam said out loud. "Somebody's goat is in our— Hey, that isn't a goat!" she screamed. She raced back to the house and burst into the kitchen. "Beauty's had her baby!" she shouted excitedly.

"So soon?" Mrs. Weirton looked stunned.

Julie just stood and stared.

"Quick. Get your coat on," Sam had to yell again before Julie started to move.

"I can't believe it. We were going to watch!" Julie said, almost panting with excitement.

"She didn't wait," Sam said impatiently.

After what seemed like forever but was actually

only a minute, Mrs. Weirton and Julie raced after Sam to the barn. The baby still remained where Sam had seen it last, standing next to Beauty on long spindly legs. With big eyes it regarded the three humans fearlessly.

"It's beautiful," Julie breathed.

"It's a little filly," said Mrs. Weirton.

Cindy rushed out of the barn, still chewing the last of her grain, and pranced nervously near the door.

"We had better watch for a few minutes to be sure Cindy is not going to bother the baby," said Mrs. Weirton. "If she does, we'll have to pen her up by herself for a few days."

"Would she hurt the baby?" Julie asked anxiously.

"I don't think so," Mrs. Weirton said. She looked puzzled. "She seems awfully nervous, though."

"I'm going to call Jazz and Sky so they can see," Sam yelled as she ran back to the house.

Only a few minutes after she returned, Jazz and her brother arrived. They were equally delighted with the new arrival. "When do you think she was born?" Jazz asked.

"I would guess early last night," Mrs. Weirton said. "She seems pretty sturdy on her feet."

"I thought you had to call the vet when a baby horse was born," Jazz said.

Mrs. Weirton chuckled. "Well, I did plan it that way. But horses have been having babies by themselves for thousands of years. I guess Beauty decided she didn't need our help after all."

"Beauty seems to be in good shape," Sky said. "But she sure hasn't gotten back her girlish figure."

It was true. The little black mare seemed as chunky as ever. She stood placidly near the baby, half asleep in the bright November sun.

Cindy moved closer to the baby, and Beauty shifted herself in front of the new filly protectively.

"I guess we don't have to worry," Mrs. Weirton said. "It looks like Beauty knows how to take care of her baby. But I don't understand why Cindy seems so upset."

Cindy circled around, trying to get close to the baby, but once again Beauty positioned herself in front. The baby took a few wobbly steps toward Cindy.

"The baby seems very interested in Cindy," said Mrs. Weirton with a puzzled expression. "Be ready to shoo Cindy away if she tries to nip at her."

At last Beauty allowed the new baby to approach Cindy. The baby nuzzled against Cindy, as though looking for food.

"You don't think Cindy would kick her or anything?" Sam voiced the fear in all their minds.

"I think we had better shut Beauty and her baby in the barn for a few days," Mrs. Weirton said. She reached for the gate to open it.

"Wait," Sky said suddenly. "There is something strange going on. Take a good look at Cindy. Doesn't she look thinner? And she isn't acting mean with the baby. She's nursing her."

"But how . . . ?" Sam's jaw dropped in astonishment.

Suddenly Mrs. Weirton began to laugh. While the others looked at her in confusion, she laughed until she was almost doubled over. When she could get her breath, she choked out, "I think we'd better hold off on that book we were going to write."

Sky was chuckling by now, too, but Jazz and Sam looked at each other, still not comprehending.

"I don't understand. Why shouldn't we write the book?" Sam demanded. She stared at the filly. "She really is nursing. Oh, my gosh!" she exclaimed. "If Cindy has milk that must mean that she is the mother."

"But I thought the vet said Beauty was going to have a baby," Jazz said weakly.

"I guess the vet was wrong," Mrs. Weirton said, breaking out into a fresh burst of giggles. "Beauty was only baby-sitting while Cindy ate her breakfast."

The sound of a car turning into the driveway made them all turn. Kevin leaped from the car, and the next few minutes were filled with greetings and hugging. Jim parked the car in the garage and joined them.

"Come and look," Sam and Julie urged, dragging Jim and Kevin to the pasture fence. Everyone tried to tell the story at once, so it took several minutes to make them understand.

"We have to get home," Sky said quietly to Sam while the others were still marveling over the birth. "There are a lot of aunts and uncles coming for dinner. Maybe I can come over tomorrow." He bent down suddenly, and his lips brushed against hers in a soft kiss. Sam touched her lips in wonder, and she looked up to see Jazz grinning at her.

"See you later," Jazz called cheerfully.

"Let's go in the house for a while," Mrs. Weirton said, putting her arm around Kevin.

Sam grabbed Jim's hands and twirled him around in a little dance. "This is the best Thanksgiving anyone ever had," she shouted.

Julie looked thoughtful as Jim nodded. "It certainly is," he said.

By the time Kevin had unpacked his suitcase

and taken a tour of the house, dinner was ready. The table was heaped with sweet potatoes, salad, cranberry sauce, peas, and freshly baked rolls. And crowning it all was a golden brown turkey packed with juicy stuffing.

"Can I say grace?" Julie asked.

"That would be nice." Mrs. Weirton nodded.

"Before I do, I want to say something I've been thinking about," Julie said hesitantly. "It has to do with Beauty and Cindy. They are kind of like a family. I mean, the baby is Cindy's, but Beauty wanted to protect her and take care of her, too." She looked at Jim. "Do you know what I'm trying to say?"

"I think I do," Jim said gently. "Beauty will be a real help to Cindy, and the baby may learn to love Beauty almost as much as her own mother."

"Families grow and change," Mrs. Weirton said, looking around the table at her family. "But our love sort of cements us together."

As Julie said grace, a warm glow settled over Sam. She knew life wouldn't stay as perfect as it was this minute, but she also knew they were on their way to being a family at last.

"Enough of this mushy stuff," Jim said, cheerfully picking up the knife to carve the turkey. "Let's eat."

"What are we going to name the baby?" Mrs. Weirton asked, passing the stuffing to Sam.

"I have an idea," Sam said, smiling at her step-father. "After dinner, why don't we make a list?"